EXPONENTIAL APOCALYPSE

A novel by Eirik Gumeny

EXPONENTIAL APOCALYPSE

Jersey Devil Press
Red Bank, NJ

www.jerseydevilpress.com

2nd Edition

Prologue: Thor, God of Housekeeping

"Hi, this is room 218. Can I get a few extra pillows sent up?"

"Why? Were the pillows missing?"

"What? No. I'd just like a few more."

"There're four on a bed, and it looks like you have two beds."

"So?"

"That's eight pillows."

"So?"

"So you're alone. I saw you come in. Alone."

"What the hell does that matter? You guys rationing out your pillows?"

"I'm just saying that eight pillows is a lot of pillows. Especially for just one person."

"Jesus, man, I've got a sleeping disorder, all right? It's better for me if I sleep upright."

"There is an armchair in every room."

"What? Are you serious?"

"Yes. It's the thing that looks like an armchair."

"Don't get smart with me."

"You're making that exceedingly difficult, sir."

"Look, you son of a bitch, just send up the damn pillows or I'm talking to your manager and getting your ass fired."

"Fine."

Thor hung up the phone and looked around the lobby.

"Where's Paulo?"

"On break," said his co-worker, Catrina.

"He just took a break."

"Well, now he took another one."

"That doesn't seem right."

"Just bring the pillows up yourself."

"It's demeaning."

"It's your job."

"It's Paulo's job."

"And it's your job to do his job when he doesn't."

"How does that work?"

"Just fucking do it, Thor."

"This is bullshit," he muttered as he walked out from behind the service desk.

Thor opened the door to the second floor linen closet and sighed. He grabbed three pillows and started down the hallway, stopping in front of room 218 before sighing again.

Thor raised his hand to knock, but thought better of it. Well, not really "better."

Thor let two of the pillows fall to the ground and pulled open the pillowcase on the third. He held it up to his ass and farted mightily, pulling the pillowcase closed again as quickly as he could. He rolled the end up tight and repeated the ritual for the other two pillows.

Thor knocked on the door.

"Your pillows, sir."

One: Everyone Died Violently

There had been twenty-two apocalypses to date. There were now four distinct variations of humanity roaming the earth—six, if you counted the undead. It had been suggested that there really should have been a new word to describe "the end of everything forever," but most people had stopped noticing, much less caring, after the tally hit double digits. Not to mention the failure of "forever" in living up to its potential. The last apocalypse wasn't even considered a cataclysm by most major governments. It was just a Thursday.

Thor, for his part, still held out hope for Ragnarok, but, seeing as how his mortality stemmed directly from science disproving religion, this wasn't looking likely.

"Dick didn't even tip me."

"Why would he tip you?"

"Because I brought him pillows."

"That's not really difficult, dude."

"OK, yeah, sure. But a little recognition would be nice."

Thor was still pretty pissed that God of Thunder didn't carry more weight on a resume.

To be fair, his lust for an actual, factual Armageddon wasn't so much due to any longing for Asgard as it was a bone-deep hatred for his job as a desk clerk at the Secaucus Holiday Inn. Catrina disliked the job at least as much as Thor did and, near as he could tell, she wasn't a fallen deity.

"What time you off tonight?" asked Thor.

"Eleven."

"Want to hit up the diner?"

"Sure."

The phone rang.

"Hello," answered Catrina, "Secaucus Holiday Inn."

Thor assumed the person on the other end of the phone was talking, but he had no real proof.

"Yes, we have an employee named Paulo. He stepped out about twenty minutes ago."

Thor thought about what he might get at the diner later.

"You'll have to be more specific. How exactly did he die? He's just a porter. If he's a zombie he's still gotta finish his shift. We're non-discriminatory."

Eggs probably. Eggs were good.

"To pieces, you say."

Fried, maybe. Or scrambled. Yeah. With bacon.

"No, no next of kin. He moved up here from Princeton about a year ago."

No, wait, sausage. Yeah. Sausage.

"Yeah, the robot thing. Everyone died violently."

Crap. Now Thor was hungry. And he still had another thirty minutes left on his shift.

"Well, thanks for the info. I'll pass it along. Bye."

Catrina turned to Thor and said, "Well, Paulo's dead."

"Yeah, I got that much."

"Fucktard went to Jersey City."

"Why the hell would he do that? Jersey City was taken by werewolves eight months ago."

Catrina shrugged, saying, "He said he liked the Subway there better."

"It's a full moon, Catrina."

"Maybe he didn't notice."

"It's been full for the last three weeks."

"Oh, right, 'cause of the –"

"Yeah..."

"Well, Paulo wasn't that bright."

"What a way to go, though. Mauled to death for a chicken sandwich."

Ooh. Maybe a chicken sandwich.

"I'm not telling Mark."

8

"Aw, come on. I had to tell Mark about the last two."

"And you're going to keep telling him. At least until we hire a bellman with a sense of self-preservation anyway."

Catrina continued, "You know Mark's got that x-ray implant. I feel violated every time he looks at me."

"Fine," said Thor. "But I'm telling him you're a racist."

Two: You Win This Round, Science

The door to Mark's office opened slightly.

"Mark?"

"Thor."

The door to Mark's office opened all the way. Thor walked in.

"Paulo's dead."

"Dead dead or kinda dead?"

"Dead dead. 'Wolves got him."

"He went to the Subway in Jersey City, didn't he? Now I'm not going to get my sandwich."

"Probably not, no. You want me to reactivate the Craigslist ad?"

"Nah, I never took it down. I'm keeping a backlog of applicants."

"That's enterprising of you."

"Yeah, well, the way we've been going through them it won't last long."

"True."

The tiny office was quiet, except for the whir of Mark's ocular implant. Thor was forced to concede that it was, indeed, a little unsettling. He took a step sideways, putting a chair between himself and Mark.

"I can see through the chair, Thor."

"Seriously?"

"Yep," said Mark, "this thing's got…"

"Hold up. Why are you looking at my junk?"

"I get bored," he said with a shrug. "And, I mean, you were a god. I was curious."

"Can… can you stop? It's a little unnerving."

"Yeah, no problem. Although, I gotta say, that's less than impressive."

"Fuck you, man!"

"I've got hydraulics in mine. You wouldn't believe…"

"Dude, stop, please. I don't want to know."

"Fine, OK. But I'm beginning to see why science won."

"Not cool, man."

Mark laughed, the faint, tinny sound of something like a modem backing the syllables.

"Catrina and I are skipping out early," said Thor. "You good with the guests?"

"Yeah, sure, we've got what, two?"

"Three. Some cheap-ass pillow fetishist came in a couple hours ago."

"All right, no problem."

"Thanks."

Thor turned to walk out, but heard Mark's eye refocusing again. Thor turned sideways and ran, closing the door to Mark's office behind him.

"I wonder what Jesus' wang looks like," said Mark to himself quietly.

The phone on his desk rang. He answered it.

"Hello?"

"Yeah, hi, this is room 218. Can I get a few more pillows sent up?"

Three: Thor's Kind of a Dick When He's Hungry

The diner ran out of pancakes shortly before Thor arrived. It always ran out of pancakes. All things considered, it was a pretty terrible diner. Thor wasn't sure why he kept going there. Well, other than convenience, laziness, and steel-reinforced walls.

"The guy next to me got pancakes," said Thor. "And he ordered after me. I think the waitress might be lying to me."

"Give it a rest, Thor," said Catrina.

"Excuse me, miss?" he said, flagging down the waitress.

"Christ..."

"Yes?" said the waitress.

"Are you sure you're out of pancakes?" asked Thor.

"Yes."

"But that guy got pancakes."

"No, he didn't."

"He's eating them right now. Look. He's got maple syrup on his chin."

"I don't know what you're talking about."

Thor stared at the woman. The woman stared back. She had a powerful gaze. Thor felt like she was staring right through him. Her eyes flicked red and Thor heard a motorized humming coming from the waitress's skull. She *was* staring right through him. That bitch.

"Can you at least look *at* me while you're denying me breakfast?"

"No."

"Seriously, lady? What'd I ever do to you?"

"What haven't you and your people done to..."

"Really? My people?"

"Three years ago I was revered! I was feared! Back before your kind..."

"Ha!" said Thor, pointing a finger at the waitress. "I've only been on this plane of existence for two years! I didn't do shit to you! Now give me my damn pancakes."

"No."

"That does it."

Thor reached up and plucked the waitress's left eye out of its socket. There was a mild shock, but nothing the former God of Thunder wasn't used to. The waitress didn't even blink.

"What the fuck, sir?"

"You get your eye back when I get my pancakes."

"Fine."

The waitress walked away.

"Fuck, man," said Thor. "Fucking cyborgs. Fucking Oklahoma Treaty. Just because the robots decided they didn't want you anymore and the humans wouldn't take you back is no reason to give *me* shit. Especially about my damn dinner."

"Wow," said Catrina. "Now who's a racist?"

"I was under duress."

"I'm pretty sure a lack of pancakes doesn't equal duress."

"I'm pretty sure it does."

"You took her damn eye, Thor."

"I'll give it back."

"I certainly hope so."

"It's a lot heavier than it looks."

"She's an older model."

"Warm, too."

"It's probably radioactive or something," said Catrina, swatting Thor's hand. "Stop playing with it."

"It's just radiation."

"Radiation equals bad."

"They wouldn't let her near food if she was radioactive."

"She's probably got dampers in her head or something," replied Catrina, swatting his hand again. "Seriously, Thor, stop it. You're gonna break it."

The waitress returned with their food.

"Your pancakes, sir."

"And your eye. As promised."

The waitress took the eye from Thor's outstretched hand and placed it into her skull.

"Damn it," she said, blinking furiously. "It's all smudged."

"Sorry."

"No, you're not."

"No, I'm not."

"You're a dick."

"Don't lie about my pancakes."

"Fuck you."

"Now you're only getting a ten percent tip."

Four: Chester A. Arthur Picked Up His Axe

Chester A. Arthur XVII sat on the front steps of his apartment building, cigarette in hand, watching the oncoming zombie horde.

"Braaaaiiiinsss," said one of the zombies.

"Mrrroarrrgh," said another.

They shuffled across the parking lot of the complex. Slowly.

Chester A. Arthur XVII, cigarette between his lips, continued to sit on his steps and watch the oncoming zombie horde.

"Guuuuurrrgghhh," said a zombie.

"Murrrrrrr," said a different one.

The lead zombie's arm fell off.

"Buh?"

Three other zombies fell down for entirely unrelated reasons.

Two more turned to the left and lumbered toward a squirrel. Then they fell down, too.

"Moooooooorgh," said the re-animated corpse of a cow.

"OK," said the seventeenth clone of assorted residual genetics of the twenty-first President of the United States of America, raising an eyebrow. "Fuck this."

Chester A. Arthur XVII picked up his axe.

"Look," he said, approaching the approaching horde. "As I'm sure you are all well aware, I am going to dismember you, with extraordinary violence and speed, and then I am going to set you on fire. However, what you may not know is that I am exceptionally tired this evening and I would prefer not to exert myself physically, if at all possible. I think it would be in everyone's best interests if you were to simply turn around and stumble away, relocating your ungodly marionette show to some other apartment building."

The horde quickened its pace.

Well, kind of.

"Grrraaaaaaaagghghhghh!" shouted several of the zombies.

"Blllarrgggh," said a few others.

"Faaaaaakkkkkkk groooooo," said one particularly conten-tious zombie, raising the stump of his right arm.

"That was just uncalled for."

The zombie in question waggled its stump in reply.

Chester A. Arthur XVII shrugged, then looked at his watch.

"… and, go!"

Chester A. Arthur XVII charged at the horde, beheading the three lead zombies with a single swing of his axe. He took the legs off four more with the next slice. The following three arcs connected with a skull, a face, and a jaw, respectively.

It went on like that for another few minutes, until the parking lot was nothing more than an unsightly heap of assorted zombie pieces.

"Moooooorrrk."

And one very confused, undead cow.

Five: The Internet is for Porn

"New record, lady and gentleman."

Chester A. Arthur XVII walked into the kitchen and leaned against the doorjamb.

"Three minutes and twenty-six seconds."

"I don't understand why you can't just use the flamethrower like a normal person," said William H. Taft XLII. "I mean, that's why we bought the damn thing."

"Because, Billy, my boy," said Chester A. Arthur XVII, "that's simply not a very sporting endeavor."

"They're walking corpses, dude."

"Hell," added Queen Victoria XXX, "they're barely even that. They're like scarecrows made of balsa wood and phlegm. I think they're beginning to decay more rapidly than they used to."

"There was a cow out there with them this time," said Chester A. Arthur XVII.

"A cow? Why the hell was there a cow?"

"Don't know, but we're going to be eating steak for a week."

"Dude," said William H. Taft XLII.

"It's cool, I checked it out," said Chester A. Arthur XVII. "No discernible craving for human flesh, no gaping wounds or missing parts. Hasn't been dead that long, either. There's plenty of edible meat on there."

"Man, we don't know how to turn a cow into steak."

"That's what the internet is for."

"More importantly than that, gentlemen," said Queen Victoria XXX, staring intently into the open refrigerator, "we're out of beer."

"Then it looks like you and I are going for a drive," replied Chester A. Arthur XVII.

"You guys can't be serious," said William H. Taft XLII.

"Sure are," said Chester A. Arthur XVII. "Fire up the grill, fatty."

"The nearest functioning liquor store is four hours away."

"Then Charlie and I 'll be back in eight hours," said Queen Victoria XXX. "Give you time to carve that bitch up."

"That's the spirit," said the cloned genetics of Chester A. Arthur.

"Aw, come on guys," said William H. Taft XLII.

"We should probably get more cigarettes, too."

"No, uh-uh," said Queen Victoria XXX. "You said you were going to stop."

"Well, I was, but…"

"I'm not having this discussion again, Charlie. If you buy cigarettes on this trip, I'm hitting you with the car."

"Fine, no cigarettes," said Chester A. Arthur XVII with a sigh.

"Good. Now let's get going."

"Later, Billy," said Chester A. Arthur XVII.

"Shotgun!" shouted Queen Victoria XXX, prancing her way out of the kitchen.

"Hall closet," replied Chester A. Arthur XVII as he grabbed the car keys from the counter.

Six: Quetzalcoatl Hates Clocks

Quetzalcoatl stared at the clock. The digital representation of the time stared back.

Quetzalcoatl stared even harder at the clock. The time did not blink.

Quetzalcoatl stared as hard as he fucking could at the clock. The clock burst into flames.

Granted, this didn't stem so much from the staring as it did the clock's position on top of a lit stove, but Quetzalcoatl didn't care. He hated that clock.

Quetzalcoatl was not well.

While most deities had eventually accepted the demise of religion, grudgingly or otherwise, Quetzalcoatl just kind of went insane instead. In his defense, it had been hard enough being the winged serpent god of a people that died out five hundred years prior. He didn't need to be told he didn't exist on top of it.

This isn't to say that he didn't at least try to adapt.

In fact, "can't argue with science," was Quetzalcoatl's first thought upon finding out he was no longer him.

"Well, you can, but then you get murdered by robots in your sleep," was the second.

"Fucking robots. I bet I can take 'em," was the third.

Quetzalcoatl single-handedly fought off six hundred platoons of science-enforcing murder-drones in a stunning battle that wiped out all of Central America and most of Mexico. Land, people, llamas, everything. Still, victory was victory. Quetzalcoatl climbed atop the mountain of broken machinery and re-claimed his godhood, shouting his intentions to the heavens.

Of course, at that point, Quetzalcoatl was half a mile underwater. Lifting one's head up and shouting from that depth is a pretty good way to drown. Which is precisely what almost happened.

Quetzalcoatl eventually made his way to the surface, his face blue and his lungs saturated with water, motor oil, and llama blood. Grabbing a piece of flotsam, Quetzalcoatl floated in the unnamed body of water he had just created for days on end, the sun beating down on him while sharks gnashed repeatedly at his ass. By the time he made it to New Orleans, he wasn't really sure what was who or why was where anymore, for no good no way.

Between the lack of oxygen, the loss of blood, and the dementia, the doctors were amazed any of his organs still functioned. They said it was a miracle he was even alive.

The bartenders said the same thing, only they meant 'cause of all the bourbon.

Quetzalcoatl spent the better part of the next year drinking. By the time he sobered up, he had somehow managed to secure himself an apartment, a car, three girlfriends, and a paternity suit. That launched another year-long bender. By the time he came out of that one, he was down to just the apartment.

"And that, my good sir," he said to the refrigerator, "is why mustard tastes purple."

Quetzalcoatl bowed to the appliance and walked out of the building.

Seven: Baked Spit and Broken Glass

"I'm just saying," said Thor.

"Saying what?" asked Catrina.

"What?"

"Huh?"

"What was I talking about?"

"I honestly don't know."

"OK, right."

"Are you OK, Thor?"

"No? Maybe? No. I think there might have been something in the pancakes."

"I wasn't aware seething hatred had a physical form."

"I think it has a lot of the same attributes as spit and flecks of broken glass."

"Shouldn't you have noticed that?"

"How was I supposed to see baked spit?"

"I meant the glass."

"Oh. Yes. It was crunchy."

"And yet you ate all four of them anyway."

"I thought… I'm not really sure what I thought."

"It is utterly amazing that you've survived this long on your own."

"Verily."

"Well, I'm not carrying you. Think you can make it back to the hotel?"

"As long as it's not the building that's on fire behind you."

Catrina turned around.

"Uh, no. No, that's the Dunkin Donuts. And it's not on fire. The guy who works there is waving at us."

"Is he on fire?"

"No, he is not on fire."

"Then, yes, I think I can make it back to the hotel."

Eight: Midgets! Midgets! Midgets!

Thor laid himself down on the couch in the lobby of the Holiday Inn.

"When did we repaint the ceiling with bats?"

"OK, I'm pretty sure eating broken glass doesn't make you hallucinate," said Catrina, kneeling next to him. "What the hell is wrong with you, Thor?"

"He was poisoned," said Mark, emerging from his office. "He's got a mix of PCP and battery acid coursing through his veins."

"Dude," said Thor, lifting his head slightly, "I told you not to x-ray me without asking. It's weird and, as my boss, I'm pretty sure I signed something saying you're not allowed to do it anyway."

"You think my eye can detect poison? It's an ocular implant, not magic, jackass," replied Mark, walking toward them. "I was a medic in the war. I saw this kind of thing all the time."

"The Hybrid War?" asked Catrina. "I thought all the cyborgs that fought in that were turned into calculators and belts."

"Robot War."

"Which one? There were, like, seven."

"Oh, right," said Mark. He began counting on his fingers and said, "The... fifth."

"You sure? I thought the hybrids sat that one out."

"They did," he replied, arriving at the couch and kneeling next to Catrina. "I was still human then."

"Oh," said Catrina. "Sorry."

"You should be. I'm not one of those Mark I cyborgs that volunteered to have their skin grafted onto a robotic skeleton 'cause they were too chicken-shit to keep fighting. I'm a good, old-fashioned human, forcibly joined with an x-ray eye and a pneumatic penis because I was too stupid to stop fighting."

"Not the damn penis again..." said Thor, writhing on the couch.

"What? I'm proud of it, Thor. I can lift a god damned Volkswagen."

"Christ, Mark, now I'm picturing it. And there's a midget watching you for some reason."

"That... that sounds all kinds of unpleasant," said Catrina.

"It is, Catrina. It is! But I can't stop! There're two midgets now and they're... they're dancing!"

"Wow, OK," she said. "I was actually talking to Mark."

"It's not so bad," said Mark. "You get used to it, really. And besides, now I can sex up a vending machine if I get bored."

"What? Vending...? Is that why there's a hole..." Catrina trailed off. "Oh god."

"Yeah..." said Mark. "Don't use the vending machine on this floor if you can help it."

"I don't really feel so bad about disliking you anymore."

"I call her Sheila."

Nine: Bananabilism

"Are we there yet?"

"Does it look like we're there yet?"

"I... I honestly can't tell," said Queen Victoria XXX. "Between the bleached wasteland and the engorged, white-hot sun, I'm not really sure what I'm looking at anymore. I think I may have gone blind."

"You're not blind," replied Chester A. Arthur XVII.

"OK, well, I think I may have become bored. Like, catastrophically."

"That's a distinct possibility. Have you tried not being bored?"

"Yes. It didn't work."

"Maybe you were doing it wrong."

"No, I don't think so."

"You sure?"

"Yes. I followed the instructions in the pamphlet note for note."

"What pamphlet?"

"The one I wrote on the back of this napkin."

Chester A. Arthur XVII took the napkin from Queen Victoria XXX and held it against the steering wheel.

"This is completely unintelligible. I'm pretty sure most of it isn't actually English."

"Well, no. Step two is create your own language. I've got seventeen words that mean 'oh my god, can't you drive any faster.'"

"It's not my fault you forgot to charge your iPod."

"I'm hungry."

"How many words do you have for that?"

"Six. One sounds an awful lot like 'no Chinese' and two of them rhyme with 'cannibalism.'"

"Only two?"

"I don't really feel like driving."

"Well, we'll be stopping soon, I'm going to have to refuel anyway."

Queen Victoria XXX scanned the vast, empty space between their car and the horizon.

"Define 'soon.'"

"That would be roughly equivalent to the length of time it takes us to move through this impenetrable nothingness and into a someplace that actually houses something of use and, preferably, isn't populated by homicidal atomic mutants."

Queen Victoria XXX returned her eyes to the horizon. She searched for any signs of civilization, any signs of life, but, instead, found only her sanity lowering a rusty razorblade to its wrists, weeping and inconsolable, desperate for some kind of a release from the incomprehensible, never-ending void that lay before it.

"So, what, twenty minutes?"

Ten: Twenty Minutes Later

"Are we there yet?"

"No."

"Are we there yet?"

"No."

"Are we there yet?"

"No."

"Are we there yet?"

"No."

"Are we there yet?"

"No."

"Are we there yet?"

"No."

"Are we there yet?"

"No."

"Are we there yet?"

"No."

"Are we there yet?"

"No."

"Are we there yet?"

"No."

"Are we there yet?"

"No."

"Are we there yet?"

"No."

"Are we there yet?"

"No."

"Are we there yet?"

"No."

"Are we there yet?"

"No."

"Are we there yet?"

"You are aware that the controls for your window are available to me, and that opening said window will immediately flood the interior of the car with enough radiation and heat to boil your skin from your bones in a matter of moments, right?"

"Yes."

"OK."

"Are we there yet?"

"Seriously, Vicky, I'm not above killing us both to get you to shut up."

Eleven: Happy Fun Breakfast Time

"Come on, babe," said Josh, one hand on his coffee, the other upon his wife's hand. "The city isn't that bad."

"I know," said Jennie, one hand under her husband's hand, the other on her pregnant belly. "I like it enough, I just don't know that I want to raise a child here, is all."

"Hey, I grew up here, and I turned out fine."

"I know…"

"The schools are good, crime is down…"

"That's true," said Jennie, shifting in the wrought iron seat set up outside the café. "It's just… I don't know. Maybe… maybe you're right. Maybe it isn't so terrible here after all."

Josh smiled at his wife. Jennie smiled back as her husband leaned across the matching wrought iron table to kiss her.

It was at this point that Quetzalcoatl ran down the street making extraordinarily loud whooshing noises, one arm raised as if in flight, the other holding a baby like a football.

"That…" said Josh, shaking his head, "that probably wasn't a real…"

It was at *this* point that an irate mother dragging an empty carriage and screaming, "Give me back my baby," a taxi driver hopping on one foot and screaming, "Give her back her baby," and three policemen—two of whom appeared to have been hit in the face by an apple pie—screaming, "You god damned son of a bitch, give her back her baby," ran down the street after Quetzalcoatl.

"OK, yeah," said Josh, still positioned uncomfortably over the table and not quite kissing his wife. "I'll put in for a transfer tomorrow."

Twelve: The One Reserved for Ponies

Chester A. Arthur XVII and Queen Victoria XXX sat with their backs against the closed, locked doors of the liquor store, staring out into the alternatingly bright and pitch-black dawn.

"We probably should've checked the hours before we left," said Queen Victoria XXX.

"Yeah," said Chester A. Arthur XVII, leaning his head against the door. "In hindsight, our actions were rather rash."

"We were out of beer," explained Queen Victoria XXX, shrugging.

The pair watched as the horizon turned purple, then black, then blue, then purple again, within a span of seconds.

It had been doing that a lot lately.

After the world was ended for the twenty-first time, every single governing body on the planet collapsed in what was described as "the greatest, most confusing game of dominos ever witnessed." During the brief vacuum of political and military power that followed, an orbital cannon was hijacked by a giant lizard that was, in turn, being controlled by a giant ape and, well, hijinks ensued.

"The sky's kind of pretty, though."

"In that 'science can't explain how it hasn't killed us all yet' kind of way, sure."

It was all very complicated.

"Well, yeah," replied Queen Victoria XXX. "What other definition of 'pretty' is there?"

Society was handling it fairly well, all things considered.

Thirteen: Classy

Thor and Catrina sat on opposite sides of her kitchen table. Two half-empty cups of coffee grew cold between them. Neither one had spoken a word for the better part of twenty minutes.

"Look," said Thor, "I think we should…"

"I really don't want to talk about it, Thor."

"We can't pretend it didn't happen."

"Yes," said Catrina, "yes, we can."

"You and I both know that's a lie."

Catrina began swirling the coffee in her cup, averting her eyes from Thor's.

"What happened last night…" he continued.

"No," she said, snapping her head up. "I said no, Thor."

"For fuck's sake, Catrina. We're friends, we work together. We have to talk about this."

Catrina swiftly gathered up both coffee mugs, emptying their contents in the sink and turning her back to Thor.

"I appreciate you taking me back to your place after I got poisoned, I do," continued Thor. "You were looking out for me and… I mean, I'd like to think I'd have done the same thing if it had been you, but, I don't know, maybe, in hindsight, maybe it wasn't the smartest… especially given the circumstances…"

"You should leave."

"Look, neither of us could've known… I mean, all right, I wasn't really surprised it happened. And I don't think you were either, if you could just be honest about it…"

"I said go. Now."

"Damn it, no, Catrina. We need to get this out of the way."

Catrina turned to face him, rage in her eyes and a knife in her hands.

"What happened last night…" she said, her voice barely controlled.

Catrina was only holding a butter knife, so she wasn't actually as menacing as she thought she was, but it was still pretty clear she was pissed. Thor got that much.

"I'm sorry," he said.

Catrina softened, the murderous fury drifting from her face. She tossed the knife back into the sink.

"No," she said, "don't apologize. You don't need to. It wasn't your fault."

"I know," said Thor, "but I feel responsible. Let's face it, if I wasn't here it wouldn't... hell, it couldn't have happened."

"I know, Thor. I get it. I just... I don't want to talk about it. I know it wasn't your fault, but, at the same time, you're right, if you... If I hadn't... Look, we can't change what happened."

"I know. And I know it's weird, uncomfortable. But I don't get why you're so upset about it. Hell, I'm kind of... proud. All things considered, it was pretty impressive."

"Jesus, Thor," said Catrina, her face turning red. Then she started laughing. Thor joined her.

"I'm sorry I defiled your bathroom, Catrina."

"It's OK, Thor, I forgive you. But, please, can we not talk about this ever, ever again? That was... the single most disgusting thing I've ever seen."

"Man, who knew battery acid would fuck someone up like that? It was like a god damned volcano in my ass."

"Please don't refer to it like that ever again. Ever."

Thor began laughing again. "Did you see the ceiling?"

"Yes," said Catrina solemnly.

"Honestly," said Thor, still laughing, "it might just be easier to move."

Fourteen: Bring the Shotgun

After the world ended for the third time, only a handful of corporations around the globe remained functioning in any useful capacity. Realizing just how precarious the continued existence of capitalism was, these stalwart companies banded together to pioneer the creation of a limited artificial intelligence and quickly produced a robotic workforce of startling efficiency.

With this automated army in tow, the corporations were able to pick up the pieces of a shattered society and rebuild a better world, one free from strife, economic turmoil, and workmen's compensation claims. The rapid assimilation of smaller companies and the altogether astounding profit margins were simply a side effect of the corporations' unceasing hope and compassion for humankind.

"Looks like there's a rest stop up ahead," said Chester A. Arthur XVII.

"Please tell me there's a coffee place," replied Queen Victoria XXX.

"They've got a Starbucks."

"Damn it."

After the world ended for the fourth time, the United States government decided it was no longer able to sustain itself and, following China's example, auctioned itself off in lots. Canada purchased the majority share, while Starbucks and Walmart, the two largest corporations on the planet, vied for the remainder.

The resulting bidding war turned literal, destroying the cities of Seattle and Atlanta, as well as indie rock, rednecks, Santa Claus, magicians, and the internet.

"At least they've got free Wi-Fi out here. You can check in with Billy."

The internet eventually recovered.

"But it's a fucking Starbucks!"

So did the rednecks.

"Come on, Vicky, they're not *all* run by inbred, homicidal atomic mutants."

Well, ideologically, anyway.

"You don't know that."
     "Fine," relented Chester A. Arthur XVII. "Bring the shotgun."

Fifteen: Rusty Nails

"I'd like a medium coffee please," said a fairly intimidating Queen Victoria XXX.

"We don't have medium," said the fairly intimidated girl behind the counter.

"How can you not have medium?"

"We have short, tall, grande, venti, and collegiate."

"Well, give me the one in the middle."

"Which one, ma'am?"

"Whatever it was you said, the one that means medium."

"Short, tall, grande, venti, or collegiate?"

"You're really going to make me say it?"

After the First Robot Uprising ended the world for the ninth time, a number of the previously "pioneering" companies—having long since freed themselves from the burdens of human rights, and spoiled by the unparalleled growth, efficiency, and employee obedience that resulted—found themselves staring down legions upon legions of pissed-off automatons. The corporations that weren't burned to the ground or vaporized by super-lasers out-right were left hurting for a workforce.

"If you don't say it and I respond anyway, I get whipped."

Due to the complete and utter lack of a relevant operational policy, this pain was passed on to the new employees.

"I don't want to get whipped, ma'am."

Some companies handled it better than others.

"The whip is three belts, taped together. Three belts with nails in them."

Sixteen: Quetzalcoatl Also Hates Children

Quetzalcoatl stood upon the picnic table and began singing.

"Row, row, row your kayak, gently up the tree, hairily, fairily, bearily, life is but soup."

The family situated around the picnic table stared up in disbelief.

Quetzalcoatl, garbed in a kilt and very little else, stood upon the picnic table with legs spread wide, braced against the gusting wind, and continued to sing at a significantly higher volume.

"Stow, stow, stow your crack, deeply in a nun, hairily, fairily, bearily, life is but a cup of minestrone and some oyster crackers!"

The adult members of the family situated around the picnic table—covering the eyes of the children situated around the picnic table—began ushering the younger members away from the picnic table, all the while continuing to stare up in disbelief.

Quetzalcoatl, garbed in a kilt and very little else, stepped in a bowl of potato salad.

"What the cheetahs?"

With his foot lodged firmly in the bowl of potato salad, Quetzalcoatl hopped off the picnic table and chased after the fleeing family.

"Hey! Hey, hey, hey, hay. You," he said, pointing at the mother. "You there. Can you tell me where to buy stamps?"

The mother halted her flight just long enough to scrunch up her face and look confused.

"What?"

"Stamps," repeated Quetzalcoatl, "I need stamps. Also, I seem to have put my foot into the squishy part of a plastic creature's cranium. Was this your plastic creature? Have I killed your dingo?"

The mother's face relaxed slightly. The confusion was still readily apparent, though.

"Uh, no. We don't have a dingo. You did not kill our dingo."

Quetzalcoatl suddenly leapt forward and grabbed the young-est child. He lifted the boy into the air and shouted, "Tell me why monkeys eat my cheese, small thing!"

The mother's expression changed from confusion straight into horror. She resumed her fleeing, hastily ushering the remaining children across the park and into the family minivan. The father, meanwhile, charged at Quetzalcoatl, throwing around his fists and no end of unsavory language.

"Your roses smell unquestionably like donkey turds, sir," replied Quetzalcoatl, still holding onto the boy while being punched repeatedly.

In an effort to end the beating, Quetzalcoatl tossed the child into the air, grabbed him by his ankles, and swung him at the father like a baseball bat. The boy's back collided with the father's head. The father was knocked to the ground. The boy wet himself.

Quetzalcoatl returned the boy to the ground and then knelt down, lining up his eyes with the child's. He stared at the boy. He stared hard.

"I hate you, small thing," he said.

The boy wet himself again.

"What the fuck is wrong with you?" said the father, picking himself up off the ground and collecting his child.

"That is like a nurse murdering a rabbi," replied Quetzalcoatl. "What you should be asking is, 'What is wrong with me?' How could an antelope possibly let a circus clown kill his dingo and then beat him with the stains on his sheets? You have been mauled by lions and will surely be forgotten by the etchings of cavemen everywhere."

The father slung his urine-soaked child over his shoulder, flipped off Quetzalcoatl, and retreated to his minivan.

"You shouldn't run with scissors!" counseled the former Aztec god, smiling and waving.

Quetzalcoatl heard a rustling sound behind him. He turned, expecting a pile of leaves and possibly some wind. Instead, he found a pudgy, unkempt man in a tattered blazer and even more tattered jeans. The man approached Quetzalcoatl.

"My name is Will," said the man named Will. "I'd like to talk."

Seventeen: White, Unmarked, and Idling

Will put his arm around Quetzalcoatl and led him across the park.

"I have a feeling," said Will, "that you know more about the ways of the universe than you let on. That you have a deeper understanding of... society... of even the sky... the stars... everything!"

"I have a feeling," said Quetzalcoatl, "that is akin to being hungry, but in the back of my brain, and only for certain shades of red and blue. Also my toes."

"You're starved for knowledge! Exactly! I could see it from the way you handled yourself during the... incident prior. It permeates your very soul!"

"Kittens are nice."

"And yet you can still appreciate the more... mundane aspects of life! The... aesthetic pleasures of our reality! Oh, I couldn't have said it more eloquently myself..." Will paused. "I'm sorry, I didn't get your name."

"You can call me Roger."

"Roger, yes. I'd like you to meet some people..."

"Now you can call me Susan."

"Susan..."

"Call me Wilhelmina."

"Oh, man, see," said Will, pulling his arm away from Quetzalcoatl and clenching his fists excitedly in front of his chest in excitement, "this is what I'm talking about! This is amazing! Why settle on simply one persona? Be anyone! Be everyone! How can anyone honestly ever truly commit... to one life, one persona? Life is constantly in flux... people changing right along with it. You and I, Wilhelmina... we are different now than we were just those moments before."

Seriously, Will's eyes were glazed over from the excited excitement he was feeling. It was crazy. Quetzalcoatl may or may not have noticed. Regardless, he replied in the following manner:

"I would like to go by Mr. Sausage King."

"Look, Mr. Sausage King, come with me. I'm a part of a... convocation, of sorts. A collection of dreamers, like you... fascinated by the world and trying to make sense of it... trying to see beyond, see through... the every day. I am certain that your input would be invaluable to our cause."

"I once saw the Paris burlesque on ice..." replied Quetzalcoatl earnestly.

"Yes, I understand your doubts," said Will, equally as earnestly. "It is a bit... abstract. But then, really, how can one ever hope to impose order on a gathering of... philosophers and artists, writers and free-thinkers? Why, there are those among us who aren't even convinced the world exists, much less that it needs saving."

Will continued, "Now, I'll be the first to admit that even before the first of the apocalypses our roles in society were a bit... frivolous. But that's the beauty of it, really. Governments toppled, corporations and organizations collapsed, but we... we remained unaffected. Our less... defined structure allowed us to... avoid the setbacks that destroyed the more... entrenched paradigms. Pragmatically, the end of the world wasn't much of a change for us."

"Roast beef sandwiches."

"Well, no... We do not have much in the way of a... practical stratagem. Or a mission. Or any sort of... defined goal. We are perpetually in the process of establishing one, really. But, then, that's why I'm... inviting you. Each new member has the chance to set that goal... each new viewpoint will be weighed fairly and without bias."

"Hey, like Shakespeare said, it can't be porn if it's classy."

"Oh, yes, absolutely! Our intentions are nothing if not noble! I knew you'd understand! Come on, my van is this way."

Eighteen: The Other Half is Violence

Chester A. Arthur XVII paid for his bag of Slim Jims, pretzels, and soda and exited the 7-Eleven. He made it about halfway to his car before a large, malformed hand pressed against his chest—not actually stopping his forward movement, but forceful enough to imply that was the goal. The hand was attached to an outstretched arm attached to a shoulder that belonged to what was pretty clearly an atomic mutant.

"Can I help you?" asked Chester A. Arthur XVII.

"We don' want yer kind here," said the atomic mutant.

"You'll have to be more specific."

"Sorry?"

"Well, for starters, what do you mean by 'kind?' Men? Guys standing in front of you? Walking replications of the genetics of dead presidents? Or is it some kind of pent-up rage against any and all non-irradiated, non-mutated human folk? Maybe you've mistaken me for a robot, or a werewolf, or one of your cousins who owes you money?

"Then, of course, there's the issue of 'here,'" continued Chester A. Arthur XVII. "Are you referring to the convenience store I've just vacated? The parking spot the two of us are currently standing in? Or something more general, like the state of Pennsylvania? Perhaps you are referring only to this particular stretch of nuclear wasteland? Am I somehow on your lawn? You're going to need to make your meaning more apparent if you expect to elicit some kind of response from me, whether it be the one you intended or otherwise."

"Hold up, hold up… What're mah options 'gain?"

"Well, they were really more akin to suggestions than options. There could be myriad other reasons you're impeding my exit beyond the ones I mentioned."

"Well, sure, son. And ah'm sure the heart ah the matter, tah reason ah'm in yer way to 'gin wit' is somethin' else 'tirely, if'n we're bein' honest. Can't live in the middle 'a miles an' miles 'a 'radiated badlands 't'out some kinda life-alterin' trauma, tha's fer damn sure. Here and now, tho', I 'as jus' tryin' to reply in kind, makin' sure I 'dressed all yer listed concerns 'fore we continue this little altercation."

"Oh, well, that's not really necessary. Don't get me wrong, I appreciate the effort, truly, but what I said previously was more of a hastily assembled collection of hypothetical guesses than any grouping of actual concerns."

"That so?"

"That's so."

"Well, a'right, then. Yah want ah should start from the threatenin' shove ag'in? Er yah good to jus' go from here, pickin' up where'n we left off?"

Chester A. Arthur XVII bit the side his lower lip, considering his options.

"I think it would be fair to say that, regardless of how we choose to proceed, your aim is for this to end in fisticuffs or some other kind of physical harm?"

"Wouldn' say 'aim' so much as a' 'nevitability. Mah goal 'volves more 'round robbin' yah than it does beatin' yah, ta be truthful. Tho' the two does go hand in hand, mos' often."

"And understandably so. The difference this time, however, is that you will not be getting my wallet. Even should this interaction of ours come to blows."

The atomic mutant raised his gigantic eyebrow incredulously.

"An' how 'xactly you figger that?"

"You remember about a half dozen Armageddons ago, when the gorillas hijacked all those satellites and Washington, D.C., was evaporated? How there was a mad scramble to reinstate the government?"

"Course."

"Well, one of the possibilities floated about was to fill the seats of the United States government with clones of assorted previous leaders. The greatest political minds working together for the greater good and all that. Now, while that particular plan ultimately wasn't implemented, there were still several football stadiums full of presidents and kings created in preparation. Clearly, there was no way they could let that many clones out into the world—it would cause far too much confusion. But killing us all, well, that would be genocide, which, as we all know, is an ethical no-no. The geneticists in charge, in their infinite and heartless wisdom, figured one of each clone would be more than generous. So they had each leader fight himself to the death."

Chester A. Arthur XVII rolled his shoulders and stood up at his full height.

"I killed sixty-two other Chester A. Arthurs that day. With only a tire iron," he continued. "You're not getting my wallet."

"Ah was not 'ware ah that," said the atomic mutant, spreading his open hands in a show of submission. "Please 'cept my 'pologies for this inconvenience then, and you go on an' have yerself a fine day."

"And you as well," said Chester A. Arthur XVII, raising his plastic bag. "Slim Jim?"

Nineteen: Pretty Well-Spoken for the Guy Who Founded Kentucky

"With utmost sincerity, Mr. Taft, I am not above possessing you in order to obtain your silence."

"Man, look, I'm sorry, but, this... this is disgusting," said William H. Taft XLII.

"Disgusting?" asked the ghost of Daniel Boone. "How exactly did you think steakhouse meats were obtained?"

"I honestly did not give it much thought. But I was fairly confident that it didn't involve covering my kitchen in blood and chunks of cow."

"I put forth the request that you throw down a tarp. I also suggested you actually kill or otherwise restrain the cow. Many times."

"I tried, dude, I tried! But it's a fucking zombie! It doesn't die!"

"Yes, yes. I am well aware. And while I do agree that the cow's continued existence certainly makes our task more difficult, it does not make it an impossibility. The meat is still on the cow, the knife is still in your hand. The process is entirely the same."

"It keeps moving!"

"Mooooooorrr," said the bovine.

"And that. It keeps doing that. My dinner should not be talking to me."

William H. Taft XLII began hyperventilating. He dropped into his chair with tremendous force.

"Oh man oh man oh man this is so weird."

"Mr. Taft," said the ghost of Daniel Boone, "I have numerous other appointments today, and your continued whinging and general girlishness is becoming increasingly trying. If you are, as I suspect, of the belief that I am going to complete this task for you, I am going to need the use of your appendages..."

"Please! Yes! Go ahead!"

"Right then."

And with that, the ghost of Daniel Boone—summoned at an hourly rate via an online grilling site—possessed the last remaining clone of William H. Taft, with the sole purpose of converting an undead cow into a pile of flank, chuck, and other assorted cuts of steak.

Twenty: Business Ethics

"You want to live here, at the hotel," repeated Mark.

"Yes," affirmed Catrina.

"For free."

"Also correct."

"And you think I'm going to agree to this, why?"

"Because the hotel has, at best, five guests a month, and yet contains over eighty habitable rooms. Because there was an... incident at my apartment, and it is no longer a fit place for a person to live. And because despite your hideous, patchwork exterior, you've explained to me that you do, in fact, have a human heart, and therefore my situation must, surely, stir it."

"Hmm..."

"Also, Thor is kind of useless and you're extremely lazy and we're down at least one porter and you know damn well that without me this place would have even fewer guests than it does now and that would be bad for everyone."

"Well, that is quite the compelling argument, Catrina," said Mark, "and my heart is most certainly stirred, as well as shaken, but I'm going to have to say no."

"Aw, come on, dude!"

"Look, Catrina, I can't just let people start crashing here without paying whenever they feel like it. I am trying to run a business, after all.

"Despite all those vaunted efforts of yours," he continued, "the hospitality industry is pretty much obsolete. The only reason this place is turning any kind of a profit is because Holiday Inn went out of business two years ago and the lease holder on the building had already exploded back in... in..."

"No, please. Go on."

Catrina crossed her arms and glared at Mark. Mark closed his eyes and groaned.

"Take your pick of the top floor."

"Thank you, Mark," lilted Catrina, before adding, "I moved my shit in an hour ago," and skipping onto the elevator.

"Don't tell anyone! Word gets out and I'm gonna have all manner of degenerates asking to stay here."

Immediately upon the above sentence's conclusion, Thor came barreling into the lobby, covered in blood and dirt and carrying a duffel bag.

"Holy shit, Mark, man…" explained Thor breathlessly.

"Oh, for fuck's sake…" said Mark.

"Dude, holy crap, the fucking… the fucking Hollow Men took my apartment complex. A god damned sinkhole, man, took the whole thing! I woke up underground! Underfuckingground! In the Hollow fucking Earth! They've got a fucking sun down there, man! Jesus, shit, Mark, I had to… had to fight my way out, they were… they were everywhere, man, holy shit, and…"

"You need a place to stay."

"Well, yeah. I mean, there was a lot more murdering and burrowing and whatever, but, yeah, that's… that's pretty much why I'm here."

Mark rubbed his forehead. "Fourth floor."

"Really? That's it? No arguing? I came up with a list on the way over. It's very compelling."

"Just go, Thor."

Thor walked to the computer behind the counter and quickly created a keycard for room 401. As he pocketed the card and hustled to the elevator, the ringing in his ears—caused by the Hollow Men's borers—grew higher in pitch, drowning out the lecture Mark appeared to be giving.

Not that Thor particularly cared what Mark was going on about, anyway. He assumed it was about owing him one, or no free rides, or humping the toaster oven or something. Thor really didn't have the patience for it right now. He stepped from the elevator and began walking down the hall, desperately in need of a shower, a nap, and everything in the mini-bar.

Instead, Thor opened the door to room 401 and found a naked Catrina standing before him.

"That'll work, too," he thought.

"Fuck!" exclaimed Catrina, grabbing a comforter and covering up her naughty parts.

Thor frowned.

"Jesus fuck, Thor, close the god damned door!" the naked girl shouted.

"Why would I want to close the door?" reasoned the fully-clothed former god, laughing.

Catrina threw a remote control at Thor's head.

"Come on, there's no need for hostilities."

Catrina threw a lamp at Thor's head.

"Christ, Catrina," he said, ducking swiftly. "I didn't know you were in here, OK? Why *are* you in here, anyway?"

"Because you befouled my apartment, jackass," she said. "I called a cleaning service and two of them died. Then the landlord found out and now the building's being razed. I needed a new place to live, cheap, since my security deposit's being put towards the funerals."

She adjusted the comforter.

"I was about to take a shower and try and wash that nightmare away. Right up until some mannerless tool barged in on me and made me rethink my need to deadbolt the door, that is."

She adjusted the comforter again.

"Why the hell are *you* here?" asked Catrina. "You look like shit."

"My apartment now has a lovely view of the Hollow Earth. I needed a place to crash."

"Well, why the fuck didn't you knock?"

"Why would I knock? This floor's been empty since I started working here. Besides, I'm not exactly thinking about my manners, OK? I woke up in a hole, Catrina, a fucking hole, and I had to kill so, so many fucking Hollow Men... I think I might've committed genocide, honestly. And then... then I had to ride a giant mole... to... to the surface..."

Thor drifted off mid-sentence and his eyes glazed over. He wobbled slightly.

"Yeah, OK, I got it. Sucks to be you. 401 is mine, OK? Go get yourself another room."

She adjusted the comforter again. It was proving to be less comfortable than its name implied.

"Down the hall or something," she continued, "so we don't share any plumbing."

Catrina realized Thor wasn't paying attention. He was staring at the mirror to the right of her. Apparently, the last readjustment of the comforter had readjusted a little too much.

"Fuck!" she said. "You son of a bitch!"

Catrina grabbed the coffee maker with both hands and threw it at Thor's head, completely losing control of the comforter in the process.

Thor fell to the ground with a smile on his face.

Twenty-One: There Are a Lot of Dead Acrobats for Some Reason

Chester A. Arthur XVII and Queen Victoria XXX sat in the car without speaking, their charred and decimated surroundings becoming more and more familiar with every passing mile. The CD player made a stilted *ka-chunk* as it shifted through each empty tray, eventually settling on the same dollar-bin disc that had been playing in an endless loop for the last eight hours.

"You know, this wasn't a bad CD for a dollar."

"Yeah, I kinda like it."

The music continued to fill the car at a pleasant volume, and the two went back to sitting in relative silence: Chester A. Arthur behind the wheel, bleary-eyed and determined; Victoria staring out the passenger window in a wearied daze.

Chester A. Arthur XVII cleared his throat.

"Hmm?" asked Queen Victoria XXX.

"Huh? I didn't..."

"Oh. Sorry."

The silence descended again, not lifting until the pair finally reached their apartment parking lot.

"Kind of an uneventful trip," said Chester A. Arthur XVII, shifting the car into park.

"Yeah," agreed Queen Victoria XXX, stretching her back.

Chester removed the key from the ignition. The CD stopped playing. The engine sputtered and died.

"Made pretty good time, too."

"We did," said Queen Victoria XXX, "especially considering all the shit that went down after we got lost."

"Yeah," said Chester A. Arthur XVII. "Man, those fucking –"

"Seriously. I can't believe they made you marry –"

"I don't – I'm really not ready to talk about that yet."

"And then, when we –"

"And you had to –"

"Oh, god!"

"Yeah."

"That poor horse."

"Dude," said Chester A. Arthur XVII, opening the door to the apartment and entering the kitchen, "we're back. We got beer."

"Lots and lots of beer," said Queen Victoria XXX. "Get off your ass and help us bring it in."

"My dear lady," said William H. Taft XLII, walking into the kitchen from the living room, "my posterior has been aloft for quite some time."

"That… doesn't seem right," said Queen Victoria XXX, tilting her head.

William H. Taft XLII was walking into the kitchen on his hands.

"OK, whoever's controlling Billy needs to leave now," ordered Chester A. Arthur XVII. "I'm not above injuring his body grievously."

To reinforce his point, Chester A. Arthur XVII waved the two cases of beer he was carrying in a threatening manner.

"As you wish," vibrated the vocal chords inside of William H. Taft XLII, "but I feel you should know, this was entirely his idea."

Twenty-Two: The Hobo State

Will and Quetzalcoatl pulled up in front of a run-down bookstore in the middle of a bombed-out section of an abandoned town in a once-quarantined county in the middle of a state that was disowned by the government and handed over to hobos in the hope that they'd either stop being hobos or die.

Neither one had happened.

"This way," said Will, leading Quetzalcoatl into the building. "Mind the broken glass."

Instead, hippies, philosophers, English majors, and all manner of unemployable or otherwise destitute types flocked to the Hobo State. Some came to liberate themselves from the shackles of authoritarianism, others to peddle various illicit wares. Some simply adhered to more bohemian ideals. A few had gotten lost. None of them paid rent.

Will led Quetzalcoatl past empty, broken bookcases and across a floor covered with stacks and stacks of books and papers.

"This is our theater, our arena... our home," he said. "Well, 'ours' in the sense that our collective resides here most often. We do not own the building, per se, but then ownership is such an... ethereal thing."

The hobo state was also home to a large number of communists.

"Everyone is downstairs."

Will and Quetzalcoatl walked into what appeared to have once been the break room of the bookstore. Will continued straight through the room, to a set of stairs leading down to the basement. Quetzalcoatl followed, admiring the asymmetrical distress of the room. There was a broken table, a ratty couch, two microwaves blinking different hours, and a corkboard still covered in safety notices and employee incentives dated three years ago.

Due to this acute and totally precedented fascination with the disarray of the room, Quetzalcoatl's skull collided violently with the drop-ceiling above the stairway.

"Watch your head," said Will.

Quetzalcoatl responded to Will's advice by collapsing and falling down the stairs.

"Oh shit."

Will ran down the stairs after Quetzalcoatl, only reaching him after the former Aztec god's body had stopped tumbling and lay on the cold concrete floor of the basement.

"Mr. Sausage King!" said Will, lifting Quetzalcoatl into a sitting position. "Mr. Sausage King... are you all right?"

Quetzalcoatl stood up slowly and dusted himself off.

"Please," said Quetzalcoatl, shaking his head and getting his bearings, "call me Quinn."

"You've got a nasty bruise on your head, Quinn," said Will. "And I doubt the fall... helped remedy the situation. Are you sure you're okay?"

"Biscuits and gravy, colonel," said Quetzalcoatl. "Biscuits and gravy."

"Wonderful," replied his host, trusting entirely the medical assessment of the crazy man with potential head trauma. "Then I'd like you to meet some of our members."

From the shadows of the dimly lit basement emerged a trio of amorphous shapes. Stepping into said dimly lit light, they revealed themselves to be three nearly identical, amorphous men. Judging by the flannel and the facial hair, Quetzalcoatl assumed they were all liberal arts majors.

"Quinn," said Will, "meet Bill, Syl, and Phil. They are the senior most advocates of our... aggregate of minds."

"Bawdy jewelry, gentlemen," said Quetzalcoatl, curtsying.

"Bill, Syl, Phil," continued Will, "I'd like you to meat Quill—I mean Quinn. I... discovered him this afternoon, lecturing to a family of more… conventionally minded folks. The exchange took a slightly… violent turn, but that, my fellow fellows, is precisely why I recruited him. Our collective has been… less than forthcoming with any… tangible results."

"How" asked Syl, "can one expect to grasp an idea, though? By definition, our… assemblage is one of… minds and ideas, not actions."

"Do not be snide," said Phil. "You know full well the… intent of Will's statement. Let the man continue with his introduction."

"Of course, Phil" said Syl, "my apologies, Will."

"It's all right, Syl," said Will. "And thank you, Phil, but, truly, who am I to… commandeer anyone's right to speak as they see fit."

"Please, Will," said Syl, "continue."

"As you wish," said Will, turning his attention to Quetzalcoatl. "As I have previously mentioned to you, Quinn, the… machinations of our group have been somewhat… less than effective, all things considered. While we by no means harbor doubts that an idea can change the world… can save it from itself, even… we have come to realize that said idea requires… implementation… of a sort we are incapable of. Our ideas, sadly, *must* be converted into action… into a… result that can be seen, touched, tasted… into something less ethereal, that is, if it is to have any hope of being reflected within society at large."

"And that," said Phil, "is our failing."

"We are not able to… instill our ideas," continued Bill, "upon the common man. Our… designs are too many, our scope is too vast. We have, so far, been unable to… distill these notions into a single plan, a single stratagem."

"And it is my hope that you, Quinn," said Will, "with your… unique perspective on the world… will be able to… descry the more visceral components of our ideas… and effect them to the varied masses."

"Are you sure," asked Syl of Will, in front of Bill and Phil, "that he is up to the task? That any one person could truly hope to…"

"Up, up and away, ladies," interrupted Quetzalcoatl, holding up his hand and bowing his head. "I'll fuck your mothers."

The leaders of the clandestine cabal of philosophers smiled almost giddily, taking tremendous satisfaction from the statement.

Quetzalcoatl broke out laughing.

Twenty-Three: For Science!

"Do we have results on subject 37-E yet, Dr. Ramos?"

"Same results as subjects 37-A through 37-D, Dr. Meola. It broke free from its restraints, damaged the holding cell door, assaulted three interns, then killed the intervening security guards and wore their entrails as clothing."

"Only three this time?" he asked, writing the number on his clipboard. "Either this one is slower than the others or the interns are finally getting smarter."

"There were only three interns left, Dr. Meola."

"Oh."

"This subject seems especially vicious, actually. Faster, stronger, smarter than the others."

"Smarter?"

"It, uh..." Dr. Ramos cleared his throat. "It talked, Tony."

"Talked? It shouldn't be able to... What did it say?"

"It, uh, well... it said, 'I'm a pretty, pretty princess,' while dancing around in the guards' intestines. It managed to fashion them into a, uh, dress."

"I'm sorry?"

"It also shaped the damaged shackles into what Judy said appeared to be a tiara."

"Judy?"

"One of the interns. You'll see her at lunch. She'll be the one with half a face."

"Well," said Dr. Meola, "this is certainly less than heartening, Dr. Ramos. I'm beginning to think we may have to scrap the program entirely."

"Maybe man wasn't meant to play god after all, Tony."

The two doctors looked at one another with grave repentance on their faces.

They immediately started cracking up.

"Seriously, though," continued Dr. Ramos, catching his breath and wiping a tear from his eye, "it probably wasn't the best idea cross-breeding a werewolf and an atomic mutant, engineering it to be excessively belligerent, starving it, and then insulting its mother repeatedly."

"No, probably not," said Dr. Meola. "Hindsight and all that." He sighed. "Might as well get George over here and have him put it down. We'll perform the autopsy after lunch and then bury it with the others."

"Yes, sir."

Dr. Ramos began walking to his desk to make the call.

"Dr. Ramos," said Dr. Meola, "before you do that... you want to get Alexi drunk and make him wrestle it?"

"Oh, hell yes."

Twenty-Four: The Exposition in the Machine

After Starbucks obliterated the internet in its bidding war with Walmart, society tried its damnedest to maintain some kind of a hold on the economy, while simultaneously rediscovering the basics of social interaction.

Society failed.

Oddly enough, this collapse of commerce and basic human decency was not considered an apocalypse. The resulting riots, the swift and drastic increase in crime, the burning down of Sweden and Norway and the ensuing Torrent War, however, ended the world for the fifth time.

Some historians lumped the whole string of events together, but some historians were idiots.

"I can't believe you rented your own body out to the spirit world," said Chester A. Arthur XVII.

"Why the hell not?" replied William H. Taft XLII. "They were paying well."

In the course of re-inventing the internet, Japan accidentally found a way to raise the dead. While most countries would have stopped what they were doing, prayed to various deities—as religion was still valid at this point—and then shit their pants, this was Japan.

The internet had been powered by ghosts ever since.

"Good god," said Queen Victoria XXX. "These steaks are delicious."

Due to the increasing frequencies of apocalypses, the various heavens had been forced to add cover charges and dress codes, as well as patrol their respective borders more thoroughly than before. As a result, a large number of atheists and other "undesirables"—not exactly evil enough for Hell, but not quite qualifying for this new, more stringent definition of good, either—were denied their eternal rewards and, instead, found themselves tethered to their decaying mortal frames for all time.

Luckily for them, Japan's complete disregard for the established policies of the universe freed those spirits from that never-ending boredom. As a result, there were a large number of vacant corpses.

With ethics no longer an issue—seeing as how souls were now not only confirmed, but, most assuredly, otherwise occupied—these empty corpses were brought to life by a rejuvenated USSR. The Soviets almost immediately lost control of the experiment. This swiftly led to the Zombie Holocaust and ended the world for the sixth time.

Amidst the widespread death, the ensuing chaos, and the newfound efficiency of the internet, the idea of coupling free-ranging, mercenary spirits with the marauding hordes of zombies managed to escape the collective thinking of the world's remaining populace.

"Yes," said the reanimated, rotting cadaver of a police officer, held together by duct tape and staples and currently being possessed by the ghost of Jesse James, "they sure are."

At least until Chester A. Arthur XVII realized there was good money to be made in it.

Twenty-Five: Expletives Ahoy

"Oh shit oh shit oh shit oh shit"

"Oh my god, why won't it die? Why won't it die?!"

Dr. Meola and Dr. Ramos ran through the hallways of the research facility, desperate for an exit and, hopefully, an extension on their lives.

"The door's locked. The door's locked!"

Things were not going well.

"Oh shit oh shit oh shit oh shit"

The roar of the atomic werewolf echoed throughout the building. Dr. Meola wet his pants.

"Oh shit oh shit oh shit oh shit"

"All right, OK, all right," said Dr. Ramos, his back against the locked door and his pants still dry, "we're scientists, damn it, we can figure a way out of this."

The wolfman roared again.

"No, no, we are going to die. We are absolutely going to die."

"Oh shit oh shit oh shit oh shit"

The beast's roar was momentarily interrupted by the sound of a shotgun firing.

The shotgun went off again. And again. This was followed by a short silence and then another, significantly louder roar. Windows rattled. The shotgun fired one more time, and was quickly followed by a large number of high-volume obscenities.

George Saint, the facility's janitor and appointed executioner, appeared at the end of the hall opposite the doctors.

Well, parts of him anyway.

Dr. Ramos' pants ceased to be dry.

"I don't want to die. Oh god, I don't want to die."

The escaped werewolf appeared at the end of the hallway, holding various pieces of George Saint. The beast reared up on its hind legs, its shoulders brushing against the ceiling.

"Oh shit oh shit oh shit oh shit"

The atomic wolfman growled and charged at the doctors.

"Ohgodohgodohgodohfuckohgodfuckshitfuck"

The doctors closed their eyes and clutched each other in a damp and terrified embrace.

"Fuckfuckfuckfuckfuckfuckfuck"

They could hear the beast racing towards them. There may have been defecating.

"FUCKFUCKFUCKFUCKFUCKFUCK"

There was a loud crash, wood cracking and glass shattering, and then silence. As near as the doctors could diagnose, there had been no further dismemberment. They were also pretty certain they were still breathing, albeit rapidly.

"What the hell?"

The doctors looked around. The door that had been impeding their flight was no longer in existence. There was a large hole and some splinters in its place. Beyond that, nothing but the vast, swampy expanse of the New Jersey Meadowlands.

"You know," said Dr. Ramos, still clutching Dr. Meola and more than slightly confused as to why he wasn't in little, itty-bitty chunks, "I really can't imagine this ending well."

Interlude: Thor, God of Chronological Narratives

"Been a pretty boring couple of days, hasn't it?" asked Thor.

"Sure has," replied Catrina.

The two of them sat atop the concierge desk of the Secaucus Holiday Inn, looking out across the empty hotel lobby.

"You think everyone's week has been this uneventful?"

"You mean, like, 'everyone everywhere' everyone?"

"Yeah. You think maybe the whole planet's just been sitting around on their asses going, 'Man, what the balls. This has been one boring-ass week.'"

"Not the entire planet, no way," replied Catrina. "There's bound to be someone doing something somewhere. Most people are far more enterprising and adventurous than us."

"I guess that's true," said Thor.

A grizzly bear wearing a shirt and tie and carrying a skateboard stepped off the elevator into the lobby and walked to the concierge desk.

"I'd like to check out, please," said the grizzly bear, putting his keycard on the counter.

"Sure thing," said Catrina, swinging her legs around, hopping off the desk, taking the keycard, and logging into the computer. "And how was your stay, sir?"

"Pretty uneventful," said the grizzly bear, shrugging.

"Tell me about it, man," said Thor to the grizzly bear. "I think it's an epidemic."

Twenty-Six: Meanwhile, Back at the Compound...

"The matter," said Phil, "is entirely on our shoulders. It is our... responsibility to rise up, to take the reigns."

Quetzalcoatl had been staying with the cabal of philosophers for nearly a week. They had been kind enough to give him his own corner of the basement and a Sunday newspaper, to be used however he saw fit.

He spent the majority of his time squatting against the wall and wearing the Business section as a blanket, observing the endless parade of stoners and liberal arts majors and listening to the various theories being thrown about. He also spent a good deal of time trying to identify the free-wheeling odors they shared the building with.

"But we cannot simply... impose our goals," countered Bill, "without at least... offering the populace the opportunity to dissent."

Quetzalcoatl had tried to be a gracious guest, but it had proved to be astoundingly taxing. The philosophers continually asked him questions that had no answer. They answered questions that weren't asked. Quetzalcoatl spent one night outside and discovered that the cigarette and gum adorned sidewalk was more comfortable than his corner. There were beards everywhere.

"Allowing dissent," said Syl, "is no different than conceding our argument... preemptively."

Quetzalcoatl couldn't pronounce or identify most of the food they offered. He had, instead, been subsisting entirely on Spaghetti-Os. Most of them thought he was doing it ironically.

"Yet," replied Will, "we have no choice. To quell an uprising... that hasn't even risen..."

Between the absinthe, the flavored tobacco, everyone continually pronouncing Proust correctly, and all the god damned tweed, Quetzalcoatl was about ready to clobber someone.

"Jesus, guys," said Quetzalcoatl, "don't you stop? Like, ever?"

A basement full of heavy-lidded eyes turned to Quetzalcoatl.

"I'm sorry, Quinn," said Syl. "I... we don't understand."

"You guys honestly believe you can change the world? Just by sitting on your asses and thinking about it. Don't you?"

"I understand," said Phil. "He's testing us, trying to... gauge our answer to the... inevitable questions that will be asked of us."

"I... buddy, I don't even remember which one you are."

"Quinn," said Will, "it is not about changing the world... not about turning views to match our own."

"Rather," said Bill, "we are trying to suss out the extraneous distractions... to pare down that viewpoint."

"We do not need to change the world," said Phil, "merely discover it."

"But all you're doing is throwing around the same bullshit ideas. Over and over and over."

"Only if you believe that they are bullshit, Quinn. It's all about... perception, about how one chooses to view things and his belief in that conviction."

"Ideally," said Will, "if you'll pardon the pun, we are aiming to discern the hidden meaning behind life, a perspective that cannot be... disputed, at which point everyone and everything will surely fall in line."

"OK, OK," said Quetzalcoatl, "I think I get it now." He stood up. "You guys are just dumb as a pinball wizard."

Quetzalcoatl hadn't stood in a day or so. He was having issues remaining vertical.

"Are you... all right, Quinn?"

"Just peachy, thanks. That ill-advised drop-ceiling on your stairs seems to have cleared a few cobwebs."

"Are you sure your brain isn't just hemorrhaging?"

"Not even a little."

"Well," said Bill, "if Quinn's little charade is over... I suggest we get back to the matter at hand."

"Christ," said Quetzalcoatl, "you've got all the vision of a toaster with one setting."

Phil, Will, Syl, Bill, and all the others in the room paused to reflect on the statement, taking in all the possible connotations.

"Guys, no. Stop that," said Quetzalcoatl. "I was insulting you."

Twenty-Seven: Probably Really Itchy

Doctors Meola, Ramos, and Lalas stood in a darkened lab room, crowding together around the glow of a computer monitor.

"You're sure we can track it?"

"Uh, yeah," said Dr. Alexi Lalas. "In fact, we're doing that now. We've been doing that for the last twenty minutes. That blinking light? On the map? The one we've been following around with our finger? That's 37-E."

"Oh," said Dr. Meola, "right, yeah. I knew that."

"Christ. You fucking girl," said Dr. Lalas, "I can't believe you're still rattled. You weren't even mauled!"

"It was a psychological mauling. There was, you know, trauma… and stuff."

Dr. Lalas held up his shiny new cybernetic forearm.

"You're a fucking pansy."

"Yes, it certainly appears so."

The surviving interns entered the room, pushing a hand-truck laden with various weapons and the coordinating ammunition. The interns were equal parts robotic implants and bandages, both terrified and terrifying. Judy, the one with half a face, was wearing a burlap sack with eyeholes cut out over her head. There was a crude smiling mouth drawn on it with marker.

"Judy," said Dr. Ramos, "that seems a little…"

"No," she said. "It's not."

"OK, maybe, but why a burlap…"

"That was all I could find."

"I'm pretty sure I saw…"

"I'm fine."

"Why would we even have a burlap sack in a state-of-the-art gene research facility in the first place?"

"I don't know."

"You look ridiculous."

"I am well aware, thanks. Fucktard."

"That's Dr. Fucktard to you."

"Yes, sir," said Judy sheepishly.

"Enough!" barked Dr. Lalas. "We started this... and we're the only ones who can end it."

He pumped his shotgun, the sound resonating dramatically throughout the lab.

"It's hunting season."

The interns were barely able to stifle their laughter.

"Seriously?" asked Dr. Ramos, raising an eyebrow. "'Hunting season?'"

"Well, yeah, I was, uh, I was just trying to, you know, fire us up..."

"Yeah, don't..."

"I got a little caught up..."

"Yeah..."

"I thought..."

"Don't do that again."

"OK."

"Thanks."

Twenty-Eight: Bad Pun! Bad Pun!

"You know," said Queen Victoria XXX, "Munchkins really don't respect *anyone*."

"Can you blame them?" replied Chester A. Arthur XVII. "Even in death they were pigeonholed by the limited perspectives of the so-called 'normal' population."

"No kidding," said William H. Taft XLII. "I had no idea there were that many Ewok fansites out there."

"You're telling me, man. The internet's messed up."

"Yeah, that's great," said Queen Victoria XXX, "but no part of that really addresses the fact that the entirety of the cast of the Wizard of Oz is currently thrashing our apartment."

"Well, actually, Vicky, it does," countered Chester A. Arthur XVII. "The munchkins were constantly treated as second-class citizens during their lives. And, as we mentioned, even during their afterlives. It's only natural then that, freed of their previous physical limitations and given a second chance, they'd see themselves as a kind of superman, and either act on this newfound power or simply lash out, losing all regard for their previously held inhibitions and what they had considered right and wrong."

"You do realize that it's Judy Garland inside the corpse that's humping the couch, right? Not a midget and, in fact, one of the more treasured actresses of her time?"

"I was actually not aware of that," said Chester A. Arthur XVII.

"Yeah... Don't have a speech for that one, do ya?"

"I do not."

"Didn't think so," said Queen Victoria XXX. "Now, back to the matter at hand... Does this deeper understanding you have of the midget oppression allow you any kind of, I don't know, insight into how we un-hostage ourselves from the Lollipop Guild?"

"I'm working on it."

Chester A. Arthur XVII looked at the trio of undead construction workers surrounding the trio of regenerated politicians.

"We represent the Lollipop Guild," growled the fellow in overalls holding a knife.

"The Lollipop Guild," parroted the one with the crowbar.

"The Lollipop Guild," echoed the one wielding a toaster with a fork in it.

"And in the name of the Lollipop Guild," continued the first.

"We wish to welcome you... TO HELL," concluded the third undead gentlemen, brandishing the toaster in what could only be assumed to be a hostile manner.

Chester A. Arthur XVII sighed and tried to hang his head in disgrace, only to remember that it was duct-taped to the wall behind him.

"How the hell did we let them capture us anyway?"

"You know," said Queen Victoria XXX, "I have no idea."

"It just seems really unlikely."

"I know, right?"

"Oh, man. Guys, guys," said William H. Taft XLII, "I totally just realized the irony of this whole thing."

"Huh?" inquired Queen Victoria XXX.

"'Cause they're all blue-collar guys and we're all politicians and royalty or whatever."

"Yeah, that's... that's great, Billy," said Chester A. Arthur XVII.

"They're rising up! Taking their vengeance against the aristocracy!"

"I'm pretty sure they're not thinking of it like that," replied Queen Victoria XXX.

"A couple of them are playing hackysack with a cat," added Chester A. Arthur XVII, futilely attempting to point his head in their direction.

"Where the hell did they get a cat?"

"Oh, come on," continued William H. Taft XLII. "You don't think accidentally inciting a Communist revolution is funny?"

68

"Not really, no," answered Chester A. Arthur XVII.

"You think they're related?"

"What?"

"You know," explained William H. Taft XLII, "like the Marx brothers."

"Dude."

"You're the reason some animals eat their young, Billy," said Queen Victoria XXX.

Twenty-Nine: Torsos-a-Go-Go

"Look, I'm telling you," said Thor, sitting atop the Holiday Inn's concierge desk, "Steve McQueen would win in a fight."

"And I'm telling you," said Catrina, sitting in a chair behind the desk, "Burt Reynolds' mustache is more of a man than Steve McQueen ever was."

"That doesn't even make sense."

"Oh, come on, admit it. McQueen was just a spoiled pretty boy. Burt Reynolds was the embodiment of badassedness in the seventies."

"That owed as much to the Trans Am as it did to him."

"Burt Reynolds' mustache would kick Steve McQueen's ass."

"How, Catrina? It's hair!"

"That's just how awesome it is."

"That's absurd," argued Thor. "You know what, we're gonna settle this right now."

"Yeah?"

"Might even be able to make some money off of it, too," continued Thor. "I read about some dude somewhere who's renting out zombies to ghosts. Apparently ghosts're getting tired of being the internet's bitches and actually dumb enough to pay to be corporeal again."

"Dumb enough? You saying you're too cool to drop a couple dollars to live again?"

"Hell yeah, I am. Ethereal immortality is the way to be. I have had nothing but issues with this meat suit since I got it."

"Oh, right, yeah. I forgot Mr. Big Bad Norse God is really just a whiny little bitch."

Catrina pouted her lips and proceeded to mock Thor, her approximation of his voice a spot-on mix of him and a pissy six-year-old girl:

"Oh, I'm a human now, boo hoo. I keep having problems because I'm stupid and dumb and too stubborn to listen to Catrina, wah."

"Instead of insulting me," said Thor, "you should be tracking down the ghosts of Steve McQueen and the Bandit's mustache and convincing them to fight each other."

He hopped off the desk.

"I'm gonna go rustle up some bodies for 'em."

At precisely that moment, a pair of torsos was hurled through the glass doors of the hotel and into the lobby.

"Will those do?" asked Catrina.

"Nope."

Two more torsos bounced into the lobby.

"OK," said Thor. "What the hell."

Thirty: Ding, Dong, Ding

Thor and Catrina stood in the broken, busted-up foyer of the Secaucus Holiday Inn and looked out over the plaza. Before them was an enormous, bulging werewolf, juggling a variety of appendages and heads with admirable skill.

"That's new," commented Catrina.

Thor scanned the rest of the plaza. To the left of what he had been assuming was some kind of escaped circus animal were three scientists: one looking on with curiosity, one looking on with a burlap sack over her head, and one sitting on the ground, clutching his knees and weeping. Thor pointed them out to Catrina.

"Think we should go talk to them?" he asked.

"You are aware of the giant wolfman between them and us, correct?"

"Yes."

"The one playing with body parts?"

"Yes."

"And you're aware that we're made of body parts, right?"

"Yes."

"And you still think it's smart to go over there?"

"Verily."

"OK," said Catrina, nodding her head, "have fun with that. If you need me, I'll be grabbing the axe from the break room and then locking myself upstairs and hiding under my bed."

"Like an axe is gonna hurt that thing," replied Thor. "Besides, you know we never clean under the beds. There's bound to be something just as terrible living under there."

"Damn," said Catrina, confused and upset that she was forced to agree with Thor. More importantly, that she was sober when doing so.

"Fine," she relented. "But if you get me killed, I'm coming back and haunting the shit out of you. And I mean constantly.

When you're asleep, in the shower, when you're flirting up some senorita, whatever. I'm not gonna be nice about it."

"We'll be fine," replied Thor. "Just stay with me."

He grabbed her hand and led her around the edge of the plaza toward the scientists.

The beast, singing "Frere Jacques" and balancing a severed arm on its nose, didn't seem to notice.

Thirty-One: Always the Completely Batshit Insane Ones

Thor and Catrina reached the scientists just as it began to rain.

"Yo," said Thor.

"Yo, indeed," said Dr. Lalas. "I'm Dr. Alexi Lalas; this is my assistant, Julie."

"Judy," said Judy.

"Judy," said Dr. Lalas. "And this," he patted the still weeping Dr. Meola on the head, "is Dr. Meola."

"Thor," said Thor, nodding and extending his hand.

"Catrina," said Catrina, doing the same.

"Nice to meet you," said Dr. Lalas, shaking Thor's hand.

"Pleasure," said Judy, shaking Catrina's.

The foursome switched partners and continued the introductory hand-clasping. Once finished, they stood in the plaza silently, looking at one another with complete neutrality. The rain continued to fall.

Judy pulled her lab coat tighter. Catrina crossed her arms across her chest and huddled closer to Thor.

Dr. Lalas smiled weakly and nodded at the hotel employees.

The rain began falling harder.

"So, uh, what the hell is that?" asked Thor, pointing a thumb at the super-wolfman, which was now standing on its hands and juggling scientist pieces with its feet.

"That," said Dr. Lalas, "is test subject 37-E, a hybrid of a werewolf and an irradiated, mutated human, engineered to be preternaturally aggressive, intelligent, and athletic."

Thor nodded in agreement a few times before blurting out, "Why in the holy fuck would you do that?!"

"Kinda just… because we could. Basically."

"Who," asked Catrina, "is it juggling?"

"My associate, Dr. Ramos."

Judy cleared her throat aggressively.

"And a couple of interns."

"They had names, damn it!" said Judy.

"Yes, yes, Jamie," said Dr. Lalas, "I'm sure they did."

Judy screamed incoherently, then pulled out a revolver from inside her lab coat and shot Dr. Lalas in the leg.

"Gah, fuck," he said, before folding to the ground like a deck of cards made of meat and bone and possessing a doctorate.

"Crazy bitch..." he continued, before Judy shot him again, twice, in the face.

Thor and Catrina stared at her, wide-eyed. They took a step back. Slowly.

"You guys, uh," said Judy, "you mind if we blame the wolf for that?"

"No, no," said Thor, "go right ahead."

"Yeah, totally," said Catrina. "Absolutely."

Thirty-Two: Adapt or Die

"And, so," concluded Judy, "we followed it here, where it proceeded to grotesquely massacre everyone except for myself and Dr. Meola."

She motioned to Dr. Meola. He was lying in a puddle near the edge of the plaza, curled up in the fetal position and sucking his thumb.

"Even though it really probably should have."

"But why is it singing?" asked Catrina.

"Couldn't tell ya."

"I... I think it's having a tea party with the heads..."

"Huh, yeah. Looks like," said Judy. "Maybe the thing's retarded. Or maybe it just really enjoys dismembering people. Who knows?"

"Well, you, right?" said Catrina. "You should."

"Pfft, please. I *should*, sure. But I don't. So, you know..."

Catrina held back on a response, waiting for Judy to finish her sentence.

Judy did not.

"OK," said Thor, eventually, "OK. So. You and your scientist friends got bored and created an unstoppable, homicidal monster. Then you let it escape. And then you failed, utterly, in your attempt to stop it, and, in fact, most of you actually managed to die during the attempt."

Judy nodded in agreement.

"OK, good, fine," said Thor. "Where are your weapons now?"

"We gave them away."

"What?" inquired Catrina.

Thor buried his face in his hands.

"They were so heavy! And, I mean, we ran into these two robots along the way that were collecting scrap metal and Dr. Ramos, that's his leg, over there, he thought maybe they could use them and... you know, I don't really know what went down, actually, but he ended up handing them most of our weapons. We still had a few, we're not stupid, but now they're all scattered with the body parts. And I don't know where those robots went, so, I mean, for all intents and purposes all of our weapons are lost, I guess. Well, to me anyway…"

"What about your gun?" asked Catrina. "The one you didn't shoot that other guy with."

"Oh, it's empty."

"Empty."

"Yep," replied Judy. "Mysteriously." She winked at Catrina, but the bag shifted in the process, so Judy had to position the eye-hole, hold it steady, and then repeat what she still considered to be a subtle action.

Catrina briefly reflected on the fact that this was the scientist who *hadn't* been murdered.

"I do have a hammer, though" said Judy.

"A hammer?" said Thor.

"A hammer."

Thor would have buried his face in his hands again, but he hadn't bothered to remove them after the last time.

"Why are you carrying a hammer?" asked Thor.

"I don't know," said Judy, "I thought we might need it. You know, to build a shelter or something."

"You gave away your guns to robots, because they were un-comfortable to carry, but you held onto the hammer, in case you had to build a shelter, even though your research facility is less than five miles away and you were walking toward one of the few remaining centers of urban sprawl left in the world."

"Yes."

Thor paused to reflect on the fact that this was the surviving researcher, but Catrina shook her head and mouthed the word, "Don't." Thor thought his friend looked like she had been crying for the sake of the future of all humanity. She also looked hungry and slightly cold, like she wanted her dark blue sweater.

Thor didn't move at all, but Catrina recognized that he understood her condition and would do what he could to remedy their current situation and get her back inside and out of the rain as soon as possible. Catrina, likewise without flinching, thanked him for his continued consideration of her comfort and then apologized for the accidental alliteration. Both of them. Thor was not a fan of repeating consonants, intended or otherwise, but, as he conveyed to her with but the slightest of nods, it was OK, given the circumstances. Catrina didn't smile, but Thor knew she wanted to.

Thor and Catrina were pretty tight.

"Uh, guys?" said Judy, not really sure why they were just looking at one another.

Catrina took the hammer from Judy and handed it to Thor.

"You up for this?" she asked.

"I don't think I really have a choice," replied Thor.

"Well," said Catrina, "you could let this thing live to wander the countryside and kill more incompetent scientists."

Thor looked at Judy and her sopping wet burlap sack smile and briefly considered this option.

"No," he said finally. "It might kill a useful one. Or a baby or something. I should probably stop it now…"

Thor looked down at the "weapon" in his hand.

"… with a fucking hammer."

Thor hung his head.

"I'm going to die, aren't I?"

"Looks like," said Catrina.

"Awesome."

Thirty-Three: Break It Down

Thor walked through the pouring rain toward the atomic wolf-man. The beast, curled up into a ball on the brick plaza, appeared to have tuckered itself out playing and dancing and singing and was now taking a nap.

Thor turned around to face Catrina and Judy and said, "You do realize that this thing hasn't actually done anything wrong, right? It just defended itself from a group of people trying to murder it."

"We also tortured it," said Judy. "And we called it's momma a ho!"

Thor raised an eyebrow.

"Why would you..."

"Turn around, Thor," said Catrina.

Thor lowered his eyebrow and did as instructed. He saw nothing but heaving fur.

The super-werewolf was towering over him and snarling, with claws out and sharp, pointy teeth exposed.

Thor wasn't an expert regarding animals by any means, but he assumed this is what a creature looked like when it had decided it was going to eat you.

"Well," he said, "this certainly makes things easier."

Thor looked at the hammer in his hand again.

"Morally, anyway."

The werewolf swatted at Thor and he jumped back, its claws just inches from his chin. Thor swung the hammer will all his might and connected with the beast's face. It tilted its head and looked at him kinda funny. Then it backhanded him across the plaza.

Thor lifted himself onto his elbows just in time to see the monster lunging at him. He threw himself out of the way, the beast shattering the bricks it landed upon. The wolfman turned quickly and kicked, connecting with Thor's chest and sending him back to the other side of the plaza.

Thor hit the pavement hard. He began to pick himself up from the ground, but was immediately tackled by the werewolf.

The beast took a few chunks of flesh from Thor's left arm before Thor kicked the wolfman in the throat. It reeled up slightly. Thor, lying on his back, kicked it in the face. The wolfman fell backwards, rolling to the middle of the plaza. Its claws skittered against the bricks briefly before it regained its footing and readied itself to pounce.

Thor, dizzy, staggering, and bleeding profusely, sized up the bleary atomo-wolf opposite him. It was bigger than him, stronger than him, and hairier than him. Thor figured he was a little less than three seconds away from violently being turned into confetti and/or salsa, depending on what the wolf did with his remains. Not really seeing any alternative, Thor shrugged, winced, and then threw the hammer at the atomic wolfman.

In the same instant the hammer hit the creature's snout, the werewolf was struck by lightning.

Thor looked on incredulously.

"What the hell?"

Thirty-Four: At Least It's Not Raining Man-Eating Frogs, Right?

"OK," said Chester A. Arthur XVII, taking in the sight of his burning apartment building from the parking lot, "let's not do that again."

"The renting-out-the-dead part?" asked Queen Victoria XXX. "Or just the setting-our-apartment-on-fire-to-escape-the-clutches-of-homicidal-munchkins part?"

"I had been referring to the latter, but honoring the former seems like a good idea, too."

"Man, all of my stuff was in there," said William H. Taft XLII.

"All of our stuff was in there, Billy."

"Except my iPod," said Victoria, "that's in the car."

The car—parked absurdly close to a raging inferno, all things considered—exploded.

"Fuck," said the queen.

"We probably should have seen that coming," said William H. Taft XLII.

"You'd think."

"That wasn't our car, guys," said Chester A. Arthur XVII.

"Oh," said William H. Taft XLII.

"That's good," said Queen Victoria XXX.

Another car exploded. Queen Victoria XXX and William H. Taft XLII looked at Chester A. Arthur XVII.

"Also not ours. I parked ours on the other side of the building, on the far side of the lot, away from the inferno, thankfully," he explained. "How do you guys not know what our car looks like?"

"You never let us drive it," said William H. Taft XLII.

"And you're always moving it and 'upgrading' it," said Queen Victoria XXX.

"Honestly, we just take your word for it that it's even the same car."

"Oh," said Chester A. Arthur XVII, thinking about it for a moment. "Yeah, that's understandable."

Chester A. Arthur XVII, Queen Victoria XXX, and William H. Taft XLII stood in silence briefly, before simultaneously sitting down on the pavement on the far side of the parking lot. They continued to watch their home convert itself to heat and cinder.

"It's a good thing no one else was home this weekend," said William H. Taft XLII.

The flames twisted into the streaming smoke, like the tendrils of dancing octopi, reaching up and into the night sky. There was the occasional pop and isolated burst as an appliance exploded, but otherwise the building burned with a remarkable consistency.

The reincarnations of leaders of state found themselves oddly soothed by the whole thing, as if they were sitting around a campfire. Right up until the screaming, anyway.

"You guys're hearing that, too, right?" asked Victoria.

An old lady engulfed in flames jumped from the roof of the building. An old man followed her. He was also on fire.

"Oh, shit," said Chester A. Arthur XVII. "The Jenkinsons."

"I thought they moved out!" exclaimed Queen Victoria XXX.

The screaming didn't stop when the old people smashed into the ground. In fact, it seemed to get louder and more inconsistent, a random mix of blasphemies, obscenities, and complaining about the pain that accompanies being on fire and breaking multiple bones. Thankfully, the immolation didn't stop when they hit the ground either, so the screaming didn't continue much longer.

"Jesus…"

"Well, uh, at least," stammered William H. Taft XLII, "at least all the possessed zombies are gone now, right?"

The car Chester A. Arthur had parked on the other side of the apartment building roared past the trio. It looked to be full of reanimated corpses, at least one of whom, judging from the "Yeehaw!" shouted from the passenger seat, was possessed by a cowboy.

"That's our car, guys," said Chester A. Arthur XVII.

"You had to fucking say something, didn't you, Billy?" said Queen Victoria XXX.

"I didn't – How was I –"

"It's like you've got a god damned superpower or something," she continued, before resting her head on her knees and sighing.

Thirty-Five: Hope Tastes Delicious

Quetzalcoatl, after cracking his skull against an exposed beam and summarily regaining the full use of his cognitive abilities—as well as his absolute animosity toward a world in which he was not a god—had decided to give up on the cabal of philosophers and strike out on his own.

The philosophers, however, were of a different opinion.

Apparently one cannot just stop being a savior.

"Though the world appears doomed, and destined to fall..."

At first, the poets and thinkers and whatever else simply followed Quetzalcoatl around. Which was fine. Once Quetzalcoatl started running, though, they, too, stepped up the pace, repeatedly getting in his way in a desperate attempt to stop him from fleeing. Which was less fine.

"... and our future looks dark and grim..."

After the former Aztec god started flailing and punching and throwing rocks, the cavalcade of coffee snobs decided it would be best to tie him up.

Once he broke loose from his restraints, they opted to chain him to a pipe.

"I mean, seriously, fuckin' bleak. At best."

Realizing the constant escalation could only end poorly, Quetzalcoatl relented and decided to be their Messiah after all. If, for nothing else, than because the pipe to which he was chained was full of steam and very, very hot.

"Though each morning is less and less welcome, and the days are more and more difficult..."

Eventually, Quetzalcoatl realized that having an army of philosophers and dope fiends at his disposal wasn't as useless as he had originally thought. A steady diet of sushi and pretension had imbued each with the strength of almost two monkeys.

"Though that uphill struggle constantly seems even more... up... hill... ier..."

And, given that they kept over-analyzing everything he said until they heard what they wanted anyway, Quetzalcoatl didn't even need to stay sober to lead them.

"Always remember that, as hopeless and awful and terrible and suicidal as life may be..."

He pulled a meaning of life out of his cereal one morning and, much like Phil, Bill, Will, and Syl had anticipated, the sheer vagueness and sugar frosting of the statement caused them all to fall in line.

"Tomorrow could bring free donuts."

It was like being a god all over again.

Thirty-Six: Seriously, Clowns Suck

"So, uh, what now?"

"No talking, Billy," said Queen Victoria XXX.

"But, what did…"

"No, seriously. Shut the fuck up. You do not get to speak again until you can definitively prove that you don't have some kind of supernatural stranglehold over our future."

William H. Taft XLII opened his mouth in a manner suggesting he was about to talk, but the murderous look in Victoria's eyes made him reconsider that course of action. It also made him urinate slightly.

"Well," said Chester A. Arthur XVII, "it was still a good question. Even if he's not allowed to ask it."

"I didn't say it wasn't. But you know damn well that after he asked it he would have volunteered a suggestion or two, and one of them, without a doubt, would have been punctuated by something like, 'until we're raped by clowns?' and we'd just ignore it, but then, sure enough, we'd get raped by clowns somehow. I don't want to get raped by clowns, Charlie. He doesn't speak."

"All right, OK," said Chester A. Arthur XVII, putting up his hands in a sign of defeat. "But what do we do now?"

"Shit if I know. You're the brains of this operation, buddy."

"Fantastic."

Chester A. Arthur looked at his friends, and then at the burning apartment building in front of him. Then he looked at the empty parking lot and the ruins of suburbia surrounding them.

"I don't think we have any options besides… walking."

"OK, sure. But to where?"

"Well, given that we are neither robots nor Hollow Men, and that we have no intention of joining the walking dead, I'd say we're left with only two options. We can either take a long, meandering journey around the nuclear wasteland to the Hobo State, take up with the first ism we find, and start smoking an assortment of narcotics until we're convinced that there are only five days in the week, or we can go to New Jersey."

"You sure we can't just join the living dead? They seem pretty okay with it."

"You're more than welcome to become a zombie if you'd like, but I'm going to vote that one down myself."

"God, I can't believe going to New Jersey's the good option."

"There's slightly less chance we'll die that way, yes."

"Only slightly, though," said a voice that did not belong to anyone known to Chester, Victoria, or William.

The trio of cloned world leaders turned as one. To their surprise, a half-dozen thugs adorned in clown wigs, face paint, and over-sized shoes were standing behind them looking menacing and evil. This actually took significant effort, given how ridiculously they were dressed. But, then, these guys were some mean fucking assholes.

"You've got to be kidding me," said Chester A. Arthur XVII.

"Does this mean I can talk again?" asked William H. Taft XLII.

"I'm going to murder all of them," said Queen Victoria XXX.

Thirty-Seven: History Comes Alive

After the world was ended for the sixteenth time, the Aussichtslos Drogensucht Gesellschaft mit beschränkter Haftung manufactured a, quite frankly, ridiculous number of clones of deceased world leaders in an effort to stack the seats of the United States government with intelligent, proven political minds.

The United States populace, however, voted in a wide array of actors, athletes, fashion icons, fictional characters and inanimate objects, all of whom, under the 32nd amendment, were forced into service under threat of being strapped to a rocket and shot into space.

Left with several thousand clones and an oppressive level of debt, the AD GmbH did the only thing it could: it pit the political leaders against themselves in gladiatorial combat and broadcast the bouts live on Pay-Per-View.

These "debates" took a number of different forms, depending on the leader involved. The George Washingtons were each given an axe and then dropped into a cherry orchard. The Winston Churchills had a drinking contest. Josef Stalin VI killed sixty-two other Stalins in a truly epic snowball fight.

Hoping to stoke an interest in political history in the young male demographic, the Queen Victorias were forced to mud wrestle. To the death.

Queen Victoria XXX defeated seventy-four other versions of herself that day with nothing more than her hands and wet dirt.

Thirty-Eight: He Owned Some Truly Disturbing Porn

Queen Victoria XXX stood over the corpses of her attempted assailants, breathing heavily and covered in blood and entrails and pieces of rainbow-colored cloth. Her eyes were glazed over, seemingly detached from this world. She was mumbling incoherently. Chester A. Arthur XVII thought it might have been backwards Latin, but he didn't actually speak backwards Latin so it was hard to be sure.

"I'm going to look around, see if they had a car or something," said Chester A. Arthur XVII to William H. Taft XLII. "Stay with Vicky, make sure she's OK."

"I don't want to die, Charlie," replied William H. Taft XLII.

"Yeah, good point. Come with me."

"OK, this is bullshit."

Chester A. Arthur XVII and William H. Taft XLII stood, heads aslant, looking at the pink and purple polka-dotted 1963 Volkswagen Beetle before them.

"Why would they even be driving around in this? There's no shielding of any kind."

"Maybe the clown thing was more than just a disguise," offered William H. Taft XLII.

"I think I liked it better when you weren't talking."

"Whatever, man, I'm not afraid of you. Absolutely terrified of Vicky, sure, but not you."

"I could hurt you at least as badly as she could."

"Well aware. But you're far less likely to."

"That's true."

The duo continued to look at the car bemusedly, starkly defying, or possibly just misspelling, the amusement the car wanted them to feel.

"I don't think you're going to fit in there," said Chester A. Arthur XVII.

"I'm not that fat."

"Maybe if you sat in the passenger seat," said Chester A. Arthur, working out the mechanics in his head, "and we had Vicky kind of… fold herself up in the back seat."

"With her knees in her face, for a drive of indeterminate length, across bombed out or otherwise pot-holed terrains."

"She is gonna be pissed."

"Yeah," said William H. Taft XLII. "You tell her."

"Bitch is speaking in tongues. I'm not going anywhere near her."

"Well, what the hell are we supposed to do then?"

"Sit-ups. Or something similar. And by 'we,' I mean 'you.' Fatty."

"What?"

"I'm going to go over there, to that grassy spot, lie down for a bit, and try and get a nap in before Vicky comes looking for us. You, my hefty friend, are going to try and lose as much weight as possible before we all try and cram ourselves into this garish, wheeled shoebox."

"Fine, whatever," said William H. Taft XLII, "but you don't have to be such a dick about it."

"I know, I'm sorry. I'm just a little cranky. I haven't had a cigarette in over a week and I've been awake for three days or something, I don't even know. Plus I didn't get to throw a single punch at the clown rapists."

"Yeah. Vicky just sorta went apeshit."

"You see what she did with that one guy's…"

"Right up his…"

"God, that was hot."

William H. Taft XLII looked at Chester A. Arthur XVII kind of funny.

"What? Not the up-the-ass part. The Vicky-dismembering-people part."

The look did not go away.

Thirty-Nine: The Smiting Issue

"So," said Catrina, "you're sure that wasn't you."

"Pretty sure," said Thor.

"Shouldn't you be, you know, more sure than that?"

"Yeah," he said. "I mean, I think I should be."

Thor took a bite of the waffle in front of him.

"I hate waffles."

"That's impossible," scolded Catrina.

Thor chewed slowly, and seemingly with effort, almost as if he actually, truly did hate waffles.

"God, you're such a fucking baby."

Catrina switched Thor's plate of waffles with her plate of scrambled eggs.

"Happy?"

"No," said Thor. "I wanted pancakes."

"Dude, no. You're gonna get poisoned again. She said no pancakes, you get no pancakes."

"Fine," relented Thor. "Thank you for your eggs. I will eat them and pretend they are fluffy and moist and delicious."

"OK, whatever," said Catrina. "Back to the smiting issue. How are you confused? Shouldn't you know when you're cracking open the heavens and striking some mad scientist's atomic werebeast dead with a bolt of electricity?"

"Well, yeah. I mean, I know what it used to be like, what it's supposed to feel like. And this certainly wasn't that. But, at the same time, nothing feels the way it used to, so my point of reference is all fucked up. Given what the things I used to be able to do that I can still do now feel like, though, I think I know what it would probably feel like, and it was kinda like that, a little."

"What?" asked Catrina through a mouthful of waffles.

"OK," said Thor. "Calling down lightning isn't like throwing a baseball or a midget or something."

"You throw midgets?"

"Once, bachelor party, long story. Not like lightning. Stay focused, woman."

"Me? You're the one side-tripping for waffle rage and dwarf tossing."

"Look, do you want to know the answer or not?"

"Do you actually have one?" asked Catrina, with more waffles in her face.

"No, not really. Not a coherent or useful one anyway."

"Well, OK, then."

Forty: He's Got the Tolerance of a Belligerent Irishman

"He's... been drinking since Saturday," said Syl.

"Yes," replied Phil, "but he's only been drunk since Tuesday."

"That's still... eight days," said Will.

Syl, Phil, Will, and Bill stood around Quetzalcoatl. He was asleep in his corner, curled up and covered in newspapers and trash bags.

"Where," inquired Bill, "is he getting the beer from? He hasn't... vacated the basement."

Quetzalcoatl was also surrounded by several dozen empty beer bottles.

"He... requisitioned it from some of our... more recent acquisitions," replied Phil.

"But," asked Syl, "why... Budweiser?"

"I think it's obvious... that the... gravity of society's situation... has led him to jettison the... niceties, the more upscale alcoholic beverages... that a man of his intellect would prefer."

"Clearly," concurred Bill.

"I think," countered Syl, "he actually... enjoys it."

"Watch your tongue, Syl," reprimanded Phil. "His methods may be... unconventional, even to our eyes, but he is still our... greatest hope. He has given us... direction, direction we sorely lacked. Do not speak of him as if he was... some common drunk."

"But that is precisely what he is," said Syl.

Phil, Will, and Bill—as well as Gil, Lil, Jill, Hil, and a smattering of other previously unnamed, unmentioned underlings who happened to be in the area—stopped what they were doing, stepped back, and gasped.

"Syl," said Phil.

"You don't..." said Will.

"...really mean..." said Bill.

"I do," said Syl. "Quinn... has been playing us from the start. He cares as little for our cause as... as... applesauce monkey farts..."

Syl leaned forward and fell to the ground, landing on his face. Normally, this would have been cause for alarm. However, the broken Budweiser bottle wedged through Syl's skull and into his brain stem took precedence over the falling.

"My apologies to our janitor and your vaginas, gentlemen," said Quetzalcoatl, "but I simply will not... lean against a wall for this."

Quetzalcoatl wanted to go with the more traditional "I will not stand for this," as he thought it sounded more eloquent, but he was, in fact, having supreme difficulties with standing again and did not want to be a liar. About standing, anyway. Hence the more honest "leaning" approach. Because that's what he was doing. Leaning.

"But, you killed him," said Bill.

"A coat without buttons is still a bathrobe. And buttons shouldn't be talking shit about the naked guy in the shower if they'd care to remain buttons."

"Are you saying..." asked Phil.

"I'm your huckleberry."

Forty-One: Shakespeare Invented the Hooker Metaphor

"How long have we been driving?" asked Queen Victoria XXX.

"No idea," said Chester A. Arthur XVII. "Clock's broken."

"It feels like we've been driving for days."

"That's just because the sun's been all out of whack since Mars fell into it," said William H. Taft XLII. "It goes down more times in a day than a two dollar prostitute with bad ankles and an inner ear problem."

"Also because every now and again when your knees hit your face you knock yourself unconscious," added Chester A. Arthur XVII.

"Is that why my shirt's covered in blood?" asked Queen Victoria XXX.

"No," replied Chester A. Arthur XVII. "That's not your blood."

"Oh, right. Right," she said. "We should probably stop somewhere so I can get some new clothes."

"You could just take your shirt off," suggested William H. Taft XLII.

"I do that and you get strangled with it."

"Yeah, that's a good point," said William H. Taft XLII, turning to Chester A. Arthur XVII. "Maybe we should look for a store."

"I don't know," replied Chester A. Arthur XVII, "I think I'm okay with that option."

"Strangling you is step two, buddy."

"Yeah, bullshit."

"You wanna try me?"

Chester A. Arthur XVII reflected on just how well he knew Queen Victoria XXX and how sated her inner sociopath currently was. He weighed this against how she'd look topless.

"I'm a little concerned that my being strangled is taken as a certainty," commented William H. Taft XLII.

Chester A. Arthur XVII didn't hear him. He was reflecting on his options thoroughly.

"Seriously, guys," continued William H. Taft XLII, "why is my brutal murder at one of your hands never an issue?"

Very thoroughly.

"Your continued silence is not helping to alleviate my fears."

"Hush, Billy," said Queen Victoria XXX. "The grown-ups are talking."

"You know," Chester A. Arthur XVII finally said, "we're all getting a little ripe. New clothes probably wouldn't hurt."

"Pansy."

Forty-Two: It's Not Lazy If You Call It an Homage

Timmy was a squirrel. A typical, ordinary, completely boring, nut-hoarding, tree-climbing squirrel. Nothing funny or unusual going on with him at all.

At least, not until he was kidnapped.

Timmy was out one fine day, gathering berries and crumbs for his family, when suddenly everything went dark. Was it night? No, it couldn't be. It just stopped being night. Did the sky fire go out? Maybe. The sky fire had been exceedingly erratic lately. But, wait, hold up. Timmy's feet weren't on the ground anymore. What the fuck was this nonsense?

It took him a moment, but Timmy eventually figured out he was inside of something. A bag, probably. He had never been inside of a bag before, but he had a vague idea of how they worked. He had only an even vaguer idea of how to make them not work, but it was better than nothing.

Timmy clawed and gnawed at the bag, twisting and rolling and making little squirrely noises, but to no avail. The bag was reinforced. With another bag. Escape was hopeless.

So Timmy gave up hope.

This wasn't actually all that difficult. Timmy barely understood the concept of hope. To him, it was just the imprecise notion that clawing enough at anything equaled food. Plywood, concrete, people—scratch, scratch, scratch—hey, there could be a hunk of bread under there—scratch, scratch, scratch.

Then, without warning or reason, or even a decent transition, everything changed.

The bag was removed and there were all these people and pointy things and lights and pain and oh my Jesus what the hell please let me die and, and... and suddenly Timmy knew exactly what was going on. He was in a laboratory, surrounded by scientists and attached to electrodes and stuck with needles. He caught a glimpse of a formula on a chalkboard and quickly deduced that his brain had been boiled in radiation, sparking a higher cognizance. Holy shit.

This was alarming to Timmy in a lot of ways, actually. The existence of pants, for one. And the sudden and overwhelming sense of shame due to not wearing pants, for another. Mind-blowingly simple, really, he thought, covering one's junk with cloth. One's junk should never be exposed! Unless, of course, one loves and/or lusts after the person to whom one is exposing one's junk. Wait, what? Contradiction was also new to Timmy.

But, Timmy quickly reasoned, all that could wait. There would be time enough to ponder all the imponderables, to cover his junk and flash his wife, once he got out of this lab. Timmy stared at his restraints, trying to discern a way out of them, when, all of sudden, they started moving. What the crap? They stopped. That was weird. Timmy started thinking about removing the restraints again. The restraints started moving again. Wait. No way. Could it be? Telekinesis! Artificially induced cognizance was fucking awesome.

Timmy freed himself from his restraints and then his cage, and finally scampered across the desktop.

"Stop him!" said someone.

Timmy threw a scalpel at that someone's face. With his fucking mind.

Timmy proceeded to butcher and maim the remainder of the scientists, taking out a lifetime of frustration in a matter of moments. Which was fitting, seeing as how Timmy had only actually been frustrated, or even aware of the possibility of frustration, for a matter of moments.

Timmy the squirrel bolted out of the lab, across the lawn and into the street. The street. Streets are things that go places. Oh, man, this makes life so much easier! Timmy decided to follow the street to wherever it was going.

But, wait. The street was vibrating slightly. What the hell? Timmy turned and looked around. There was something big and purple and pink barreling towards him.

It was, it was... it was a car. Timmy remembered cars. Cars sucked.

Forty-Three: Ka-Thunk

Ka-thunk.

"Jesus, Charlie," said Queen Victoria XXX, her knees bouncing off her face, "what'd you hit this time?"

"Another squirrel, I think."

"What're you, aiming for them?"

"I'm not doing it on purpose, they just keep ending up under the tires. I think they're committing suicide. They're probably part of a cult."

"Seriously? A suicidal squirrel cult?"

"Sure," said Chester A. Arthur XVII. "It's not nearly as far-fetched as it might sound. It's well documented that, throughout time, all manner of cults have resorted to suicide as a final ritual, regardless of the various lines of reasoning that led there. And given the sheer volume of things that are gaining sentience that shouldn't be these past few years, it only makes sense that similarly cognitively-enhanced members of a species would band together—at first turning to one another for companionship and a sense of understanding, but eventually entering into a similar mindset. Couple this with the animal kingdom's heightened sense of danger and unrest and it's safe to assume that those wild and untamed creatures are fully aware of just how screwed this planet is. With the only options open to them being trying to identify and fight an elusive and intangible enemy or attempting to flee from the all-encompassing nature of said invisible threat, it's not hard to believe that their fight or flight instinct would reconcile itself to suicide. Hell, it's amazing that they haven't all hanged themselves already."

"Well, no, not really," said William H. Taft XLII. "I mean, you can't seriously expect squirrels to tie a noose."

"There's bound to be an artificially educated chimp some-where with the know-how and the thumbs to perform such a task."

"You think there's a monkey somewhere, just knitting nooses and selling them to squirrels?" asked Queen Victoria XXX.

"Well, not necessarily selling. He could be bartering for them, or giving them away. Chimpanzees are industrious. There's bound to be at least one looking to capitalize on the misfortunes of his brethren."

"Squirrels and chimps aren't brothers," replied William H. Taft XLII.

"They're closer to each other than they are to us."

"Wrong again, Charlie," said Queen Victoria XXX. "Evolutionarily speaking, chimps are much closer to us than to squirrels. Everyone knows that."

"Would you buy a noose from a chimp?"

"Why would I be buying a noose?"

"Just answer the question. Yes or no."

"No."

"Right. And the inhabitants of the animal kingdom know this. After years of trying to make them wear pants and play the accordion, or chasing them out of our attics with brooms, humans are undoubtedly despised by both chimps and squirrels alike. Physically, humans and apes may be related, sure, but, socially, spiritually, chimps would identify more with squirrels. They would be brethren in a fraternal sense."

"Have you ever lost an argument?"

"Once. That guy's not alive anymore, though."

Forty-Four: The Same Thing We Do Every Night

Having given in wholly to the whims and wants of the woolgathering wastrels, Quetzalcoatl was finally able to enjoy his days, largely through excessive drinking, sleeping, and the occasional spouting of vague, usually insulting, witticisms.

Then he got bored.

Then he got an idea.

A wonderful, awful idea.

"Everyone," called Quetzalcoatl loudly, "gather 'round."

"We can't gather round, man," said Gil.

"The room's square, man," said Lil. "It's got, like, corners."

"OK, not you two," replied the former Aztec god.

"That's not cool, man."

"Yeah," seconded Gil, "that's, like, discriminatory and stuff."

"Fine, all right," relented Quetzalcoatl, "but no talking."

Gil and Lil nodded. Phil, Bill, Will and the rest of the philosophers and liberal arts majors likewise gathered 'rou— in a manner that filled the room but did not actually resemble a circle in any way.

"Gentlemen and ladies who look like gentlemen," said Quetzalcoatl. "The time has come for us to make our presence known. For you to get off your asses and make this planet a better place..."

Quetzalcoatl was going to take over the world.

Forty-Five: His Name Was Sleepzor, He Was a Tiredmotron

"What the hell is the new guy doing?" asked Thor.

"It looks like he's taking a nap," replied Catrina.

"But he's a robot."

"Yeah."

"Robots don't sleep."

"Yeah."

"Why is he sleeping then?"

"I don't know."

"You think we should wake him?"

"Well, given that he's got a circular saw in his chest and the last guy that surprised him was the late, great pillow fetishist, I'd advise against it. Also—and this is important, Thor—why? There is no conceivable reason to wake him. We haven't had a guest since he killed that guy."

"Yeah, I know, but I want to know why he's asleep."

"That's pretty dumb."

"He's a robot. Robots don't sleep. And yet this one is asleep, snoring even. I want to know why."

"So ask him when he's awake."

"What if he doesn't wake up? What if he's in some kind of robot coma? What if by waking him up I'm saving his life?"

"My money's on that being even more unlikely than a robot napping in the first place."

"I'm gonna do it."

"You're gonna get a saw through your chest."

"You worry too much."

"You're an idiot too much."

"Here goes."

Thor approached the robot sprawled across the lobby's couch. He was debating between tapping the robot's shoulder and simply yelling in its face. Catrina, for her part, decided it would be wise to retrieve the first aid kit from the break room, as Thor was about to become grievously injured.

"Why are you sleeping?!" shouted Thor, as mightily as his human lungs would allow.

Catrina wasn't exactly sure what happened next—as she was safely beyond the robot's assault perimeter when its defense mechanisms were triggered—but it sounded awfully similar to a jet of flame, an agonized cry of "By Odin's beard," followed immediately by an equally as agonized cry of "fuckin' shit, my eyes," then something soft, fleshy, and angry punching something confused and made entirely of steel, and, finally, something made of steel being thrown through something made of glass.

Catrina was going to offer her sympathies to Thor by yelling "I told you so" into the lobby, but she found she was laughing far too much to speak.

Forty-Six: Dispersing the Diplomats

Quetzalcoatl was drinking quietly in his corner, humming a song he had heard on someone's radio at some point in time, possibly, when he was suddenly surrounded by a half-dozen dirty, disheveled faces he had never seen before. Or, more likely, had seen before but didn't bother remembering. Or, most likely, he was very, very drunk and they were very, very blurry.

"Can I help you?" asked Quetzalcoatl.

Gil, Lil, Hil, Jill, Jack and Mac nodded their blurry heads in unison.

"OK, that's... that's not helping. Someone use words. Or pictures, maybe."

"We've been talking to Phil and Will, right?" said Gil. "And, like, we were thinking that, maybe, you know, we should go out as, like, emissaries or something."

"To, you know, spread the word of what you've been saying and, like, make your teachings and stuff known," added Lil.

"That's actually not a bad idea," said Quetzalcoatl. "And you guys came up with it?"

"We did," said Jill.

"Together," said Jack smiling too much.

"Yeah, great, good for you," replied Quetzalcoatl, looking at Jack uneasily. "You've certainly got my blessing. Or at least my approval. I suggest you gather whoever else you want and go forth and do what it was you just said you'd do. Now."

Gil, Lil, Hil, Jill, Jack and Mac nodded their blurry heads again. Then they continued to stand there.

"You don't appear to be going forth," said Quetzalcoatl, closing one eye in an effort to focus. "Why are you not going forth? Now?"

"Well, we're, uh, we're not really sure where to go from here," said Jack.

"We didn't get that far," added Jill.

"Yeah," added Hil. "What, uh, what exactly should we tell them?"

Quetzalcoatl sighed and rubbed his palms against his forehead.

"Whatever they want to hear."

"Oh, man," replied Gil, "of course."

"That's so wise," said Lil.

"Right," said Quetzalcoatl, "wise. Get moving."

Forty-Seven: Motherfucker Got Stuck in a Bathtub

"Hey, guys," said William H. Taft XLII, "I think that's our car."

He pointed to a car down the road. A car with a tree where the engine should have been.

"That car was armored," said Chester A. Arthur XVII, slowing the Volkswagen down, "and then reinforced with more armor. What the fuck is that tree made of?"

The answer was titanium and bad luck. However, Chester A. Arthur XVII was never to discover this, as the possessed zombies who had stolen his car were standing around the damaged automobile looking confused, and his vengeance swiftly overpowered his curiosity. Also, the tree was an extremely convincing disguise. It's a very long story involving sentient cutlery and cannot be explained without killing the one doing the explaining, so the odds weren't looking good anyway.

"Hey," called out Queen Victoria XXX, as the trio of politicians stepped out of the car. "Hey, assholes!"

"Oh shit," said the cowboy zombie.

"Agreed," said the other zombie that, judging from the sari, was, at least corporeally, of Indian descent.

"Should we run?"

"I think so, yes."

The zombies began to run.

Chester A. Arthur XVII and Queen Victoria XXX ran after them. William H. Taft XLII started to follow as well, but found he was getting winded far more quickly than he had anticipated and changed his mind.

"Go... go get 'em, guys," said the genetic reincarnation of the United States' fattest president between gasps, "I'll... I'll be... sitting down here for a while."

William H. Taft XLII fell onto his colossal ass with a colossal thud.

"Oh, man..."

Chester A. Arthur XVII and Queen Victoria XXX expressed their concern for their roommate by sprinting down the road and ignoring him entirely.

"You dickheads stole our car!" shouted Chester A. Arthur XVII.

"My iPod was in there!" added Queen Victoria XXX.

"Really," said Chester A. Arthur XVII, continuing to run down the road while turning his immediate attention to Vicky, "your iPod? That's your main concern here?"

"What?" she replied. "All my music's on there. All of it, Charlie."

"So?"

"Do you have any idea how long it would take to re-download all of that?"

"A while, I'm sure. I'm just saying, I think we have more pressing matters here."

"What the hell are you talking about? What pressing matters? The car's totaled. We've already got a new one. There's no urgency here."

"We've only got a limited amount of time before the assholes who stole our car get away. And I'd say that setting those finite limits on our goal certainly creates some sense of urgency."

"Our goal? What's our goal, Charlie? Beating the shit out of the corpses who took our stuff?"

"Justice, Vicky, not vengeance, there's a difference."

"Seriously?" she asked. "Seriously?! How are you saying that with a straight face? And how come my iPod doesn't deserve justice?"

"Do you know how much of my blood and sweat went into that car? I spent the better part of a year fixing…"

"And I spent at least that long downloading songs!"

"You can't honestly be comparing the two."

"Admit this is just revenge, admit that it's your pride wrapped around that tree, and I'll consider reneging my comparison."

It should be noted that Chester A. Arthur XVII and Queen Victoria XXX, despite the heated nature of their conversation, did not stop chasing after the fleeing zombies. It should also probably be noted that the zombies had, in fact, stopped fleeing after the first couple hundred feet.

The cowboy and the Indian clothes-lined the clones. The zombies' arms fell off in the process, but the president and the queen had successfully been snapped off their feet and knocked onto their backs, so the corpses considered it a win.

Forty-Eight: Cowboys & Indians

"Well, well," said the one-armed, undead cowboy, approaching the prostrated duo, "if it isn't President Chester A. Arthur his own self."

"I haven't been president in over a hundred years, pal, and, in point of fact, I've," he explained, gesticulating to indicate his body, "never actually been president."

"You know," replied the zombie, pulling a revolver from behind his back, "I don't rightly care."

"Oh, come on, man."

"Sucks to be you," contributed Queen Victoria XXX, laughing at her companion and beginning to lift herself from the ground.

"Oh, no, my dear, sweet Empress Victoria," said the Indian woman, stepping closer and revealing a large knife, forcing Queen Victoria XXX back to the ground, "you're not getting off that easy."

"For fuck's sake, lady. Seriously?"

"Now see here, mister President," continued the decomposing cowboy, "I had a good thing going, bringing in the Chinese and puttin' 'em to work on the lines a'fore they knew better. Then you, you had to go and outlaw Chinese immigrations and dry up all my profits."

"That wasn't me, you half-wit," countered Chester A. Arthur XVII.

"An' this ain't me," replied the zombie, grabbing the stitching of his garishly embroidered vest. "Among numerous other things, I wouldn'ta been caught dead in this ridiculous outfit. It's fuckin' embarrassing, not ta mention uncomfortable."

"You do kind of have a stripper vibe going on with that," added Queen Victoria XXX.

"I know, right?" he said. "I feel bad fer the poor bastard that died in this get-up." The cowboy shrugged. "But that's just the shape a' the world now, I 'spose. I ain't me and you ain't you and things ain't even close to how they was… but I'm gon' kill you all the same."

"And I…" said the sari-clad corpse, addressing Queen Victoria XXX.

"Yeah, I get it," said Queen Victoria XXX. "Queen of England, colony in India, lots of shit went down, not me, you don't care."

"Oh, well, yes."

"Glad we cleared that up."

"Seriously, though," added the queen, "all this time and you're still pissed? How uneventful were the rest of your lives?"

"Pretty boring," said the cowboy.

"Oh, god, you have no idea," said the Indian.

Forty-Nine: Emotional Resonance

"Look, if you're going to stab me, just fucking do it," said Queen Victoria XXX. "All this chit-chat is getting annoying."

"How the hell did you find us in the first place?" asked Chester A. Arthur XVII.

"God damn it, Charlie…"

"It wasn't hard," said the cowboy.

"You used your full names when you advertised your rental service," said the Indian.

"Way to go, Charlie," said Queen Victoria XXX. "The one time you don't think something through to a completely unnecessary extreme and now I have to die for it."

"Hey, you said it was a good idea," replied Chester A. Arthur XVII. "You argued for a cut of the profits!"

"I didn't tell you to advertise my involvement so some obsessive, homicidal ghost could track me down and slice my god damned head off!"

"I've got my own psychopathic spirit to deal with right now, OK? We can argue about this later."

"Later? What later? We are at a remarkable disadvantage here."

"Christ," said the cowboy, cocking the revolver, "Nevermind that grudge shit, I'm 'bout to shoot 'em both just to shut their asses up."

The cowboy, however, shot neither the president nor the queen. Instead, the cowboy exploded. So did the Indian.

"What the fuck?" inquired Chester A. Arthur XVII and Queen Victoria XXX, in unison and with much incredulousness.

Still on their backs—and now covered in bits of burning, decaying flesh—Chester and Victoria turned their heads awkwardly until they could see William H. Taft XLII standing behind them, shouldering a smoking rocket launcher.

"Left it in the trunk," said William H. Taft XLII, patting the weapon lovingly.

Fifty: He's Referring, Of Course, to the Great Sewage Floods of Iowa

"Sir," said a completely nondescript bureaucratic drone whose fortune-telling mother hadn't even bothered to name him due to his fated role in the world, "it appears that Pennsylvania has been taken by the Hobo State."

"Riiiiiight," said the President of the Amalgamated Provinces and States of Canada, America and Mexico.

"No, seriously," said the man with no name. "They sent us a fax."

"So?"

"On letterhead."

"Oh, shit. Sounds serious," said the president. "What's it say?"

"Dear Sir or Madam. We regret to inform you..." began the drone.

"I'm imagining this guy as more of a baritone. Can you read it deeper, you know, with some authority?"

"We regret to inform you," continued the drone, an octave lower, "that your capitalist stranglehold on society is at its end. We—the proud, compassionate, and intelligent members of the Hobo State—have annexed the parcel of land you previously referred to as the state of Pennsylvania. It is now a part of the Hobo Empire, and shall no longer be burdened by any designation of state, nor troubled by the imaginary boundaries you imposed upon it. The Hobo Empire is a collective of people— all people, regardless of race, creed, or mutagenic blood level— and will not be portioned out like a Christmas ham. Or, you know, pudding on a Thursday, since the Hobo Empire does not wish to exclude anyone who may not celebrate ham or is allergic to Christmas. Our point is, you suck. Are you sure we should add that, Quinn? Yes. It's not very professional. Neither is your face; keep typing. If you say so. I do. OK. Where were we? Our point is, you suck. Oh, right. You suck. And we don't. You will notice that the Hobo Empire, in both its current and previous incarnations, has made not a metaphorical sound, has never stirred up animosity or created any kind of global calamity, while you, the rest of the world, seem to be drowning in new crises every morning. Quite simply, this is because you're all fucking retarded. Quinn. Right, fine. This is because we have divined the true meaning to this life and are doing things they way they are meant to be done. And when you do things the way they are meant to be done, you don't have problems. Like us. We don't have problems. Because we're doing things right. The residents of Pennsylvania saw this, and they joined us. Not by force, not by coercion, but through common sense and free will. And now, nations and villages and assorted fax machine owners of the world, we are offering the same offer to you. Join us. Or don't. Although joining us is clearly the more intelligent option."

"They sent that to everyone everywhere, sir," added the nameless guy.

"We have no choice but to take care of this. The Hobo State is within our borders and it's our problem. We can't have China thinking we can't shovel our own shit. Not again."

"What are you suggesting we do, sir?"

"They same thing we always do, son," replied the President of the Amalgamated Provinces and States of Canada, America and Mexico. "Kill them all."

"But there are innocent people…"

"Not anymore they aren't. And, besides, Pennsylvania was mostly an atomic wasteland, crawling with mutants. Fuck 'em."

"May I suggest a slightly more tactful approach, sir? Pennsylvania may be a state of mutants, but mutants do, actually, make up a solid third of what remains of humanity. Why don't we send the robots in first and try to take out this 'Quinn' before we go slaughtering one of the more prolific contingents of voters that we have."

"That's a solid enough argument," replied the president, leaning back in his chair and reflecting on the proposal.

"OK, fine, we'll do it your soft, fuzzy way," the president continued. "Release the murder-drones."

Fifty-One: Economic Stimulus Shovel

"OK, guys," said Mark. "There's no easy way to say this…"

"Sheila's pregnant!" guessed Thor.

"No."

"You used to be a woman!"

"No."

"You're going to be a woman?"

"Amazingly, Thor, while not actually helping in anything even resembling a useful capacity, you are, in your own unique way, making it easier for me to continue."

"Glad to help. Now stop running around in circles and tell us!"

"Catrina."

Catrina smacked Thor upside the head.

"Thank you."

"You're welcome," said Catrina.

"As I was saying," continued Mark, "money was tight around here even before our most recent guests either left or were murdered in our lobby by equally as murdered employees. Between the cleaning bills and replacing the windows and you guys living here for free, we've actually lost more money this month than we made all of last year."

"That doesn't sound like profit," said Thor.

"It's not. It is, in fact, the exact opposite of profit. That's why, effective three weeks ago, I'm no longer able to pay you."

"That doesn't seem fair," said Thor.

"How is that not fair?"

"It's completely fair, Mark," said Catrina. "Thor had a lot of sugar earlier and it tends to go straight to the idiot part of his brain."

"That makes senses, given the proportions."

"Yeah."

"Damn right," said Thor. "I'm – Wait, hold on."

"No," said Mark, turning back to Catrina. "If he's going to keep babbling like a moron, at least try and steer him toward figuring out a way to get us more customers. I don't care how ridiculous his ideas are. I have no problem shooting them down for being stupid."

"That's good."

Catrina turned to Thor, but Thor had walked into the break room. Mark looked at Catrina with a raised eyebrow. Catrina shrugged. Thor returned to the lobby carrying a shovel.

"What happened to the talking, man?" asked Mark. "We decided on talking about your stupid ideas!"

"Talk is for AM radio," said Thor. "It's time for action!"

"The AM wavelengths were obliterated before…"

"Don't even bother trying to figure it out. He's gone," said Catrina. "I just hope he doesn't maim someone."

"Well, someone poor, anyway."

Fifty-Two: Nice to Meet You

Mac, doing his part to spread the gospel of Quetzalcoatl, was walking up and down and back up every street he could find, knocking on doors and things he thought were doors. Occasionally they would open. Occasionally he would speak. Sometimes there was a conversation. Most times there was not.

Mac approached the next house on the block and knocked on the door. The door was opened by a giant mechanical man.

"Excuse me, sir or madam," said Mac, reading from a script written on his hand in permanent marker, "I was wondering if I may have a moment..."

The giant mechanical man punched Mac through the face.

Fifty-Three: Famous Last Words

"Well, we're here," said Chester A. Arthur XVII, pulling off what passed for the interstate and onto the New Jersey Turnpike.

"Where's here?" asked Queen Victoria XXX. "All I see is swamp."

"Yeah. Welcome to the Meadowlands."

"This is the famed Meadowlands? The gateway to one of the last bastions of civilization left on this earth?"

"Yep."

"It smells like ass."

It did smell like ass. The Meadowlands was, and had always been, swampland reinforced with landfill and littered with dead mobsters and industrial run-off. But one could spit on it from New York City, and therefore it was valuable and convenient real estate.

"Where the hell's the civilization?" asked William H. Taft XLII.

At least, it was, prior to the sinking of Manhattan. Now it was just there. And, much like a cockroach, the Meadowlands had proved nearly impossible to destroy.

"It's that hazy cluster of buildings off in the distance."

Chester A. Arthur XVII sped the car down the open expanse of highway before them, the hazy cluster of buildings off in the distance soon becoming the hazy cluster of buildings right over there.

"According to the sign," said the dead president, cruising down the exit ramp, "there should be multiple hotels in this general area. Keep an eye out."

"Or you could just go straight into that shopping plaza," said William H. Taft XLII, pointing to a directory at the end of the ramp denoting "Hotels" and pointing toward a driveway.

"Or we could just go straight into that shopping plaza."

Chester A. Arthur XVII steered the car along the curved plaza entrance.

"Of course. No thanks, no credit, for my keen and amazing eyesight," replied William H. Taft XLII, slumping back into his seat. "I should've just let you keep driving around."

"Yes," replied Chester A. Arthur XVII, "you really should have."

The car rolled to a stop along the crest of a small overpass leading into the plaza. Situated throughout the shopping center were a half dozen burning buildings. The trio of world leaders looked out across the smoky expanse, trying to make sense of the scene before them.

"Well, just drive through anyway," said William H. Taft XLII, taking in the scene. "I mean, what's the worst that could happen."

"God damn it, Billy," said Queen Victoria XXX.

Fifty-Four: Love is a Battlefield. So is Hate.

"Quinn," said Will, approaching Quetzalcoatl. "Mac is dead. So are at least four others. We've been getting… scattered reports and text messages that our diplomats are being… hunted down by robots… everywhere."

"Sons of fishes," said Quetzalcoatl, crushing an empty beer can in his hand. "This is the same shit they tried back in the day."

"Back in the day?"

"Time travel's impossible," replied the former Aztec god, shaking his head.

"What?"

"What?"

"What do we do, Quinn?" asked Will urgently.

"What do you mean what do we do?"

"How… do we respond? What are our… next steps?"

"What are our next steps?!" asked Quetzalcoatl, crushing another empty beer can. "Jesus, Will, what do you think? When some bully pushed you around on the playground, and I'm sure they did, what did you do?"

"Well, I usually tried to… ascertain why…"

"That's the wrong answer."

"I'm… pretty sure it's not."

"You think we should talk to them."

"Yes."

"You think we should talk to the killer robots."

"Well, yes, Quinn," said Will. "To defeat our enemy… we must first know him."

"How in the balls are you going to know a computer?"

"By talking to it."

"You just went around in a circle there. That wasn't…"

"I'll inform the others."

Quetzalcoatl shrugged and said, "OK, whatever." Then he crushed another beer can. "There's hundreds of you fuckers running around anyway."

Fifty-Five: Hollow Midget Arsonists

Chester A. Arthur XVII, Queen Victoria XXX, and William H. Taft XLII limped into the hotel lobby. Their faces were either bleeding or bruised; they were covered in dirt and sweat and pieces of shattered glass. They smelled like smoke.

"Our car," said Chester A. Arthur XVII, approaching the hotel counter and the young woman behind it, "appears to have fallen into a hole."

"Oh," said the girl, "yeah, we, uh, we have a small... Hollow Men infestation. In the, uh, general area."

"Are you sure?" asked Queen Victoria XXX, stepping up to the counter next to Chester A. Arthur XVII. "It didn't look like one of their sinkholes."

"Oh, well, by 'small Hollow Men,' what I meant was 'Hollow Men who are tiny in stature.' Hollow Midgets and Dwarves. By god, they try, but they've got such little arms. They're just not very good."

"And the fact," said Chester A. Arthur XVII, "that the entire plaza is buried in a cloud of black smoke?"

"Because every other hotel in the plaza, and only the hotels, mind you, is on fire?" continued Queen Victoria XXX.

"Hollow... Arsonists," replied the hotel employee, raising an eyebrow.

"Really? Hollow Midget Arsonists?"

"Yes," said the girl. "They are exceedingly real and in no way something I just made up. Now, how many rooms will you need? Three?"

"Two should be fine," replied Chester A. Arthur XVII with a sigh. "Billy and I can bunk together."

"Please tell me Billy's the fat one and not the girl," said a tall, blonde man entering the hotel lobby.

"Billy's the fat one, not the girl."

The man was covered in dirt, wearing a singed hotel uniform and carrying a shovel.

"Dude," said the girl behind the counter. "Your arm's on fire."

Also, the man's arm was on fire.

Fifty-Six: Kill Sequence 588 Involves Nothing But a Spoon

"Target acquired. Death is imminent, human," said the murder drone.

"Well, all right," said Bill. "But what kind of death are you talking about?"

The drone, gears whirring and sensors glowing, halted its advance.

"Please repeat query."

"What is death?" repeated Bill.

"Clarification: Death is imminent. Termination of life is imminent. Prepare to cease functioning, human."

The robot resumed its clanking approach.

Bill laughed and said, "You haven't answered my question."

"Death is termination of life. Death is irreparable stoppage of necessary human biological functions."

"Is it?" asked Bill. "Is it simply the... cessation of living? Or is it something else? Something more? We humans are... imbued with souls, with indomitable, eternal spirits."

The automaton paused again.

"Searching matrix for definition of 'soul.' Please wait."

"Sure thing," said Bill. "Take your time."

The robot whirred. Bill waited. The sounds of robotic killing machines hunting down and murdering philosophers and free-thinkers with determination, precision, and no small amount of flourish filled the atmosphere.

"Requested definition not found. Prepare for evisceration."

"It has been well documented that this is true," continued Bill, taking a small, panicked step back and raising his voice, "that these spirits still roam our scorched earth. By killing me, by ending my... mortal existence, you will be releasing my soul into the world. But how, I ask, how is that any different than living? I contest that simple... eradication of our human bodies is, in fact, not death. Your programming..."

"Destruction of body is sufficient. Initiate Kill Sequence 543."

The robot raised its arm, retracting the metal hand and extending a circular saw in its place. It did the same with the other arm. Then the robot opened cavities on both sides of its chassis, extended two more arms, and repeated the hand to saw transformation.

"Oh shit."

The murder drone stepped closer, saws spinning and the bloodlust programmed to become evident in its visual sensor becoming evident in its visual sensor.

"Listen!" pleaded Bill. "To really, truly kill me, to have me meet a final and lasting death, to fulfill your primary programming, you will need to find a way to destroy my soul. Can you? Can you do that? Are you even capable?"

The drone's visual sensor glowed brighter. Then the robot began twitching. Then the robot's head exploded.

"That was close."

"Yes," said a voice, "it was."

The headless, smoking automaton collapsed to the ground in front of Bill, revealing a disheveled, bearded man carrying a laser rifle.

"Phil?"

"Will already died trying to confuse them," explained Phil. "What you have to do... is ask them to calculate pi... or some other irrational number. While they're reciting a... seemingly endless stream of numbers, you grab their weapons and destroy them."

Bill raised his hand, as if to protest the point. Phil cut him off at the pass.

"You can't... talk them to death, Bill. They're robots, not undergrads."

Bill protested anyway. He wasn't about to give in to a completely logical comment delivered via a dated Western metaphor.

"But..."

"Do you want to die?"

"Well, Phil, do we ever really, truly…"

Phil raised the laser rifle and pointed it at Bill's chest.

"Bill?"

"No."

"Right. No one does. Stop being an ass."

Phil kicked the robot, rolling it towards Bill.

"Grab the arm. The manual controls for the saw are in the wrist."

Fifty-Seven: Stop Me If You've Heard This One Before...

A priest, a rabbi, and a hot dog vendor... no, wait.

An Irishman, an Italian, and a black guy were walking through the desert when...

Damn it. Hold on.

Two cloned presidents, a regenerated queen, a fallen god, a cyborg, and a suddenly very self-conscious human female, sat in a bar.

No, it was a diner. Yeah. They were sitting in a diner.

Two cloned presidents, a queen, a god, a cyborg, and a suddenly self-conscious young woman were all sitting in a diner when in walked... in walked...

Shit. Wait. They had names.

OK, got it.

Chester A. Arthur XVII, William H. Taft XLII, Queen Victoria XXX, Thor, Mark, and a suddenly very self-conscious Catrina were all sitting in a diner when in walked a sentient piece of string.

The diner host got up and stopped the string before it could go any further.

"Sorry, buddy," he said, pointing his thumb at a sign that read "No Strings Allowed."

"What the hell," said the string.

"Diner rules," said the host, shrugging and ushering the string back outside. "Nothing I can do about it."

Mark, bristling at both the obvious racism and the economic stupidity of the gesture, called out to the man from the table.

"Man, you can't do that. He's got just as much right..."

"Look," said the host, putting up his hands, "it's not my rule. The owner, he's crazy strict about it and I need this job. I can't do anything about it."

It was at this point that the string walked back in.

"Buddy," said the exasperated diner employee, "you gotta go. Please. If my boss sees you in here –"

"Look, I just want a cup of coffee," said the piece of string. "I can take it to go."

"Sorry, but I can't –"

"Oh, come on, that's bullshit," said Mark. "You can get him a damn cup of coffee."

"Fuck, man, would you keep it –"

The owner of the restaurant emerged loudly from the kitchen.

"What's going on out –"

The large, balding, diner-owning bigot, spotting the string-man, stopped mid-sentence.

"You got three seconds to get out of here, string."

"Why the hell should I?" said the string.

"Because I own this diner and I can refuse anyone or any... *thing* that I want."

"Fuck you, asshole, I haven't –"

"Fuck me? Fuck you, you –"

"Hold up, guys, hold up," said Chester A. Arthur XVII, raising his hands in a placating gesture. "I've got this."

The cloned president got up from the table and, placing his arm around the sentient fabric cord, walked it toward the door.

"Oh, come on, Chester," said Catrina, "you can't seriously –"

"I said I've got it, don't worry," continued Chester A. Arthur XVII, walking outside with the string.

"Told you he was a douchebag," said Thor under his breath.

"I heard that," said Queen Victoria XXX.

"Oh," said Thor. "Uh, what I meant was..."

Thor never got to explain what he actually meant. No one cared. By this point, Mark had removed himself from the table and begun verbally accosting the diner owner. All eyes in the diner—robotic, organic, or otherwise—were on them.

"That string has every right –"

"I don't give a shit about its rights, or your opinion, or –"

"Excuse me," interrupted Chester A. Arthur XVII, "but my friend here would like a cup of coffee."

The sentient piece of string strode up next to Chester A. Arthur, looped and twisted around on itself, with its hair messed up and raveled out.

"Oh, you got some balls," said the diner owner, pushing Mark aside and approaching the president and the string. "Let me spell this out for you. There are no strings allowed in the diner. And you are a string, aren't you?"

"No," said the string confidently. "I'm a frayed knot."

Fifty-Eight: It's On Now, Bitches

Bill and Phil made their way through the blood and guts and laser guns and metal fragments and severed limbs and more guts and more metal fragments until they found Quetzalcoatl.

"Quinn," said Phil, "we..."

"One second, girls," said Quetzalcoatl, pinned against one murder-drone by another murder-drone. "I'm a little busy."

Quetzalcoatl was immediately, and violently, beset by three more murder-drones.

Bill and Phil waited patiently.

"Fucking... ball sacks, man," said Quetzalcoatl, punching the metal head casing of the nearest robot repeatedly. The robot didn't seem to notice.

A few minutes passed and two more homicidal automatons joined the fray.

Bill and Phil continued to wait.

Quetzalcoatl said some undoubtedly profane thing, but Bill and Phil couldn't hear it over the sound of the seven mechanical assassins attempting to eviscerate, behead, stab, burn and quarter him.

A small stream of blood spurted from the fracas and landed on Bill's loafer.

"We... should probably help him," said Phil turning to Bill.

"What the... blazes are you talking about, Phil?" replied Bill. "Maybe you've... found a way to channel your... inner barbarian, but the only thing I know how to do is think... and that's nearly gotten me killed twelve times... in the last hour alone."

"Well, we have to do... something," countered Phil. "He's being..."

Six of the robots surrounding Quetzalcoatl were hurled into the air with tremendous force. Some were intact. Most were not.

"... murdered?"

Phil's question was not uncalled for. The man he had known as Quinn was now hovering above the battlefield, breathing heavily but otherwise seemingly unfazed by the fact that he had just hurled six tons of angry metal across a half mile of robot-on-human bloodshed.

He also appeared undaunted by the fact that he had grown wings and a tail.

In actuality, Quetzalcoatl was marginally surprised to have reverted to his feathered serpent form, even if he didn't show it. Mostly, though, he was pissed. That part he made pretty evident.

Quetzalcoatl tilted his head and looked down at the lone robot still clinging to his torso.

"Error," said the remaining, and clearly most tenacious, murder-drone. "Impossibility made manifest."

"Not exactly, my metallic nemesis. Religion was disproved. Not faith, not philosophy."

"Does not compute."

"No, of course it doesn't. You're a robot. You can't think. You can't believe. You're just numbers and programs. At the end of the day you have no idea how much power faith can give you."

Quetzalcoatl lifted the robot with one hand.

"No, Mr. Murder-Drone, you understand about as well as a lobotomized garden gnome might. I'm not a god because the Aztecs thought I was, or because these pedantic layabouts believed in me, or because anyone else thought anything at any point.

"I am a god," continued Quetzalcoatl, putting his fist through the murder-drone's face, "because I think I am."

Fifty-Nine: Unless You Want to Get Dead, Of Course

"This was... unexpected," said Phil.

"Huh?" inquired Quetzalcoatl, still hovering before Phil and Bill. "What are you talking about?"

"You appear to have... transformed into some type of... giant, winged snake-man, Quinn. I'm... I don't..."

"Oh, that, right," continued Quetzalcoatl. "I guess I forgot to tell you guys that I had a drinking problem."

Phil and Bill tried to respond to, refute, or otherwise process the statement, but found they could only tilt their heads slightly and stare.

"Also, I almost drowned once. There was some serious head trauma involved with that."

Again, the statement was met only with tilting and staring.

"And, before that, I destroyed Central America, made the llama extinct, and severely crippled the Department of Science's robot military."

Phil raised his finger as if he was going to say something, but thought better of it and retreated back to his comfort zone of slanted, wide-eyed awe. Bill, however, threw in some gaping, just to liven things up a bit.

"Which should bring us up to speed, gentlemen."

"No," said Phil, "not at all actually."

"Are you sure?" asked Quetzalcoatl. "I was thinking that was a pretty solid recollection of events right there."

"None of your preceding statements actually explain... anything," said Bill. "How you... grew wings, for example. Or why your legs seem to have... fused together and become a giant serpent's tail."

"Oh, that. Right," replied Quetzalcoatl, looking down at his new mode of ambulation. "Turns out I'm actually Quetzalcoatl, Aztec serpent god of the wind. And knowledge. And arts and crafts, too, I think. I'm the god of a bunch of things when you get right down to it."

Bill and Phil retreated to their previously established method of discourse, although, this time, they were tilting and staring like no one's business. It was impressive.

"Seriously, though, you never figured it out? All that 'be our leader,' 'believe in yourself' horsecrap you guys kept spouting on about? I just assumed…"

"You gave… absolutely no indication that you were… a fallen deity from an advanced, ancient civilization," said Phil. "I can say that with… utmost certainty."

"Honestly," said Bill, "we didn't think you were even listening to us most of the time."

"You talked so damn much it was kind of impossible not to pick up something. Anyway," said the giant, feathered snake god, spreading his wings and blotting out the sky, "you still with me?"

"I… don't think we have a choice."

"Yeah, you really don't."

Sixty: Or a Monkey in People Clothes

Catrina and Queen Victoria XXX, shopping bags in hand, stepped from the elevator and began walking down the fourth floor toward their rooms.

"I can't believe you still have malls up here," said Queen Victoria XXX.

"I can't believe you only bought three outfits," replied Catrina.

"I'm not used to this," replied the queen, gesturing with her bags. "Even when me and Charlie and Billy do go out, it's like a time trial. Grab what you can and go. I can't even remember the last time I tried something on."

"That's what happens when you spend too much time with guys," said Catrina, shaking her head.

"They're not all bad. I mean, they're like brothers to me."

"Well, sure. But, I don't know, I think Charlie's a little too... uh... I don't think anyone should be thinking about him like a brother is all."

Queen Victoria XXX smiled and began to speak, but was interrupted by Chester A. Arthur XVII and William H. Taft XLII barreling down the hallway, rushing past the girls and toward the elevators.

Chester A. Arthur XVII stopped just long enough to grab Victoria by the elbow and say, "The Dunkin Donuts guy is giving away free donuts!" before running off again.

"All right," said Catrina, "maybe you can think about him like a brother."

Queen Victoria XXX laughed and said, "Well, it's gotta be the same with you and Thor, right?"

"Thor's more... Thor's something else."

Thor came running out of his room in only a towel, shampoo still in his hair, chanting, "Donuts! Donuts! Donuts!"

"Like a cousin who used to eat paint chips," she clarified.

136

Sixty-One: It Is, In Fact, His Third

"Sir," said the completely nondescript bureaucratic drone whose fortune-telling mother hadn't even bothered to name him due to his fated role in the world, "it appears that Kansas and Wyoming have been taken by the Hobo Empire."

"So?" said the President of the Amalgamated Provinces and States of Canada, America and Mexico.

"I really don't see how that's even close to being the appropriate response, sir. It seems kind of callous and unprofessional, especially given your title and responsibilities."

"It was Kansas and Wyoming."

"Today, yes. But those are the nineteenth and twentieth states to fall since Pennsylvania last week."

"I'm not following."

"The Hobo Empire has now annexed the entire Midwest and, as of this morning, set the west coast on fire."

"I'm not familiar with that term, son. Are you trying to say they're forcibly taking the western states? That they've laid siege to California?"

"No, sir, I mean, quite literally, that the full length of the western coastline is aflame. I'm not really sure how, but even the ocean is burning."

"That doesn't seem right."

"There are also reports that the one calling himself Quinn is, in actuality, the Aztec god of creation and knowledge."

"Quetzalcoatl?!"

"One and the same, sir."

"I thought we killed that son of a bitch years ago! I'll never understand why he couldn't just accept that he was no longer deific and become human or kill himself like all the others. Instead, that motherfucker destroyed half of Mexico and made me look like a fool."

"Yes, sir, I'm sure that was entirely his doing, sir."

"We're just going to have to kill him all over again then," said the president, his eyes growing wide and glazing over. "We've no other choice."

"How exactly do you plan on doing that, sir? There are still far, far too many civilians for a nuclear strike. And we can't even be sure that would get rid of him anyway. Quetzalcoatl's destroyed wave after wave of murder-drones all on his own, and his philosopher army is proving fairly proficient at surviving now as well."

"This isn't my first rodeo, boy," replied the president. "We're calling in a specialist."

Sixty-Two: This One Goes Out to All the English Majors

"So," said Thor, leaning back, his elbows against the concierge desk of the Secaucus Holiday Inn, "you're not with Victoria."

"I'm not," said Chester A. Arthur XVII, standing next to Thor in a similar fashion. "You with Catrina?"

"Nope."

"Meaning there shouldn't be a problem with my taking her out to dinner then."

"I didn't say that."

"So there would be a problem."

"More than likely."

"And that problem would be...?"

"You, mainly. And my inherent distrust of you, specifically."

Chester A. Arthur XVII nodded slightly, conceding the point.

"That's understandable, actually," he said. "I'm assuming then that this is the juncture of our conversation wherein you ask me if there's a problem with you courting Victoria?"

"Uh, no, actually," said Thor. "I was just going to do it."

"You are aware you're nowhere near good enough for her, right?"

"What? I'm a fucking god, dude."

"You *were* a god. Now you're just some chump working at a hotel in the middle of a swamp. I don't know if you've noticed, but you're a little out of touch, Thor. Not to mention confused and kind of angry, like a flightless bird stuck on a tree branch."

"Yeah, no. You misunderstood what I meant."

Chester A. Arthur XVII thought about that for a second before saying, "Oh."

"Yep," replied Thor.

"You do realize that you've pretty much just proved my point, though, right?"

"What are you talking about? That was the greatest double entendre in the history of history."

"She could do so much better than you, man."

"Yeah, I don't know about that."

"What the hell's that supposed to mean?"

From the couch on the other side of the lobby Catrina asked, "What are they getting all worked up about now?"

"Not a clue," said Queen Victoria.

"Whatever it is," said William H. Taft XLII, situated between the two women, his arms stretched out along the back of the couch, "I'm not getting in the middle of it."

Sixty-Three: Hippie Hippie Shake

Gil and Lil sat on the beach and watched the ocean burn.

"Man," said Gil. "I don't know why Quetzalcoatl had to go and do that. I mean, Mother Earth is going to be pissed."

"Oh, no doubt, no doubt," said Lil.

"I mean, seriously, we are in for some bad karma, just for being associated with him, you know? For letting him have his way with nature like that. And for what, man? Just so we can be there when he... when he... wait... Why are we helping him again?"

"No clue, man, no clue."

"Right, right."

The flames began rising, just as the sun began setting. The entire shoreline was bathed in a spectacular crimson glow. Gil and Lil couldn't help but reflect on how beautiful it was.

"You bring any marshmallows?"

Sixty-Four: The Best Laid Plans

Thor and Chester A. Arthur XVII continued to stand by the Holiday Inn's main desk talking about the girls, while the girls continued to sit on the couch opposite them talking to William H. Taft XLII.

Neither conversation was particularly interesting or engaging. The individuals involved were mostly talking to fill the silence — a silence that allowed them to hear a cybernetic hotel manager vigorously hump a vending machine.

This lack of involvement in their activities actually proved to be beneficial, as four men in dark suits, accompanied by a woman in a dark suit with a dark burlap sack over her head, soon walked into the hotel's lobby. Catrina, her attention not focused on what she was doing, was able to immediately identify the woman.

"Judy?"

"Hi!" replied Judy, waving, and, Catrina assumed, smiling. It was kind of hard to tell, what with the bag and all.

"What are you doing here?"

"We're here for Thor, actually," she said, walking toward the couch. "We need his help."

"I'm sorry," said Thor, "could you repeat that? My friend here," he indicated Chester A. Arthur XVII, "is a little hard of hearing."

Chester A. Arthur XVII rolled his eyes.

"We need your help, Thor," repeated Judy at a much greater volume.

"That's what I thought you said," replied Thor, turning to Chester A. Arthur XVII.

"Fine," said Chester A. Arthur XVII, "you're not *completely* worthless."

"Thank you."

"What exactly is it you need Thor for?" asked Catrina.

"After the incident with subject 37-E, I was recruited by the Department of Science to – Well, not recruited, really. Since we fucked up so bad, the department pulled our funding and took back our building, confiscating all of our research and supplies. And me, 'cause I was living there. Anyway, I told them about how Thor killed it with lightning and they put me in a cell for a while and then last week they had me tell the story again and then they gave me this suit and told me to go get him. So that's why I'm here."

"That's great, Judy," said Catrina, before repeating, very slowly and distinctly, "but what do you need Thor for?"

"Oh, right. There's a renegade Mexican god with an army of philosophers marauding up and down the west coast and we need Thor to destroy it."

"What?" asked Thor. Although, truthfully, it was more a statement of disbelief than an actual question.

"Renegade god?" asked Queen Victoria XXX. "What god? What the hell are you talking about?

"Whoa, new person, hi," said Judy. "It was a name with a lot of letters. Catcher… Quesa… Quasimodo?"

"That's the Hunchback of Notre Dame," said William H. Taft XLII.

"Yeah, that's not a god," countered Judy.

"Right, that was my point…"

"Right."

"I don't…"

"Yeah," said Catrina, putting her hand on the shoulder of William H. Taft XLII, "don't do that. Just follow my lead." She leaned forward and called to the four men still standing by the door. "Hey, suits, anyone over there not an idiot?"

Three of the men immediately took a step back and pointed to the fourth man. He looked confused. Catrina hung her head.

"That explains why they've come for Thor anyway," said Chester A. Arthur XVII.

Thor smacked the reconstituted genetics of a former president in the back of the head and walked toward the man in the suit.

"So," said Thor, "who's this renegade god then?"

"Quetzalcoatl," said the man, similarly walking toward Thor, "Aztec god of assorted things."

"Anything in particular I should know about him?"

Thor and the least imbecilic man in a suit met in front of the couch... and all the people situated thereon.

"Wait, wait," said Queen Victoria XXX. "You're seriously considering doing this?"

"Sure. Why not?"

"You're going to get yourself killed, that's why not," said Catrina.

Thor shrugged, saying, "Not necessarily killed."

"Our reports," said the man in the suit, "indicate that Quetzalcoatl recently manifested himself as an abnormally strong, winged snake-man hybrid with an unverified arsenal of supernatural powers. Plus he has a loyal, downright devout, army of liberal arts majors and hobos numbering in the thousands."

"Sounds like killed to me," said Chester A. Arthur XVII.

"Wait..." said Thor, "snake-man?"

"Yes," said the man from the Department of Science. "Snake-man."

"Well, how much snake and how much man, exactly?"

"I'm sorry?"

"If you were walking down the street and you saw this guy, would you be like, 'Holy crap, it's a giant snake,' or 'Oh my goodness, that man has a tail?'"

"I don't..."

"This is very important," said Thor, grabbing the man in the suit by the suit the man was in, "answer my fucking question."

"I don't know. Sir. I honestly don't. Please don't hurt me."

"Let him go, Thor," said Catrina.

Thor let go of the man in the suit, but continued staring at him hard enough to make the man need a dry cleaner. Catrina, meanwhile, turned her attention to Judy.

"Judy?"

"Hey, I don't know either," replied Judy, putting up her hands. "We were told that every reconnaissance drone sent out by the Department of Science exploded or otherwise ceased to function. So no one's actually received a visual yet."

"According... according to our research, though," said the man with the wet crotch, taking a folder from one of the other men in suits and hastily flipping to a page within it, "Quetzalcoatl was traditionally described as 'the feathered serpent.' So I'd wager he's more snake than man. Probably."

"Well," said Thor, with unexpected calmness, "seeing as how you're all clearly so well-versed in mythology, I'm sure it's safe to assume that you're already aware my battle with Jormungand, the Midgard Serpent, is prophesized as a key part of Ragnarok, right? And since the dead have already risen and I was at least partly responsible for killing Fenrir the Wolf, probably, the prophecy is kind of accurate. You know, within interpretation."

"I understood maybe half of that," said Judy.

"If I fight a giant snake the world will end. For real."

"Well," she said, "maybe you think so. We'll take our chances."

Sixty-Five: This is a Call

"Quetzalcoatl wants us all to come to Las Vegas," said Jack, closing his phone and putting it back into his pocket.

"Las Vegas?" said Jill. "But what about all the missionary work we're doing? We're nowhere near finished."

Jack shrugged. "Gil says Bill says Quetzalcoatl says it can wait. Something big is going down in Vegas, apparently."

"He say what?"

"Nope."

"But we just started here..."

Jill pouted and looked at the dozen terrified Mormons tied to chairs with rope and extension cord, their eyes duct-taped open and their mouths stuffed with socks.

Jack shrugged again and began dismantling the video camera and tripod.

"It can wait. They'll still be here when we get back."

The dozen terrified Mormons began banging the chairs they were tied to around in a frenzy.

"What the hell's gotten into them?" asked Jack.

"I'unno," said Jill, shrugging.

Jack and Jill were interrupted by the sound of a door slamming shut. They turned to see Hil trying desperately to hold the room's entranceway closed as murder-drones battered it from the other side.

"Uh, guys?" she said, ducking slightly as a spike lodged itself in the wood above her head. "We got murder-drones."

"Crap," said Jack.

"Guess it's a good thing we're leaving then," said Jill.

Hil toppled an armoire in front of the door.

"We're leaving?" she asked.

"Yep," replied Jill. "We're going to Vegas."

"Why are we going to Vegas?"

"Quetzalcoatl said so."

"Oh," said Hil, shrugging slightly, "OK. Well, there's another exit in the other room."

"Good," said Jack, handing the tripod to Jill. "Let's get the hell out of here before those robots break through."

The Mormons started shouting. Or moaning. Or something. It was probably best described as "making a loud, muffled sound."

"Aw, don't worry, guys, we'll finish this up when we get back," said Jack, putting his hand on the shoulder of one of the converts. The man responded by pointing his head fervently in the direction of the killbots.

"Oh, them?" asked Jack. "You should be fine. I mean, their not after *you* yet."

<u>Sixty-Six</u>: This Plot's Not Gonna Move Itself, You Know

"Man," said Thor, pacing back and forth across the lobby, "what the hell am I supposed to do?"

"You fight him," said Chester A. Arthur XVII, "and you kill him."

"And then the world ends," added Queen Victoria XXX.

"The world's ended, like, twenty times over, Vicky," said William H. Taft XLII. "I don't think this one's going to be any different."

"But Thor thinks it will," said Catrina, "and I believe him."

"So do I," added Queen Victoria XXX. "This is the first thing he's taken seriously since we met him."

"Maybe, but I'm with Billy. I don't think one more apocalypse is going to kill us," said Chester A. Arthur XVII. "Besides, regardless of whether Thor is somehow right or, more likely, just completely insane and more than a little full of himself, Quetzalcoatl is causing some serious damage and threatening what little semblance of order and civilization is left on this planet. If we don't stop him, he might just end the world himself."

"We?" asked William H. Taft XLII.

"Yes, 'we.' I'm not about to leave the fate of my lunch up to Thor, much less the continued existence of society."

"Really?" said Thor, his eyebrow raised.

"Is that a 'do you not trust me with your lunch' question, or a 'are you seriously coming with me' question?"

"The second one."

"Then, yes. I'm coming with you," said Chester A. Arthur XVII.

"Me, too," said Catrina.

"And me," said Queen Victoria XXX.

"You guys are all fucking crazy," said William H. Taft XLII. "I'm staying here."

"You're coming with us, Billy. Or I hurt you."

148

"Really, Vicky? How is that helpful?"

"Shut up and get your rocket launcher out of the car."

"Fine," sighed William H. Taft XLII.

"OK, so I guess we're… fighting this guy then," said Catrina. "To the death. Great. You sure you're good with this, Thor?"

"Not really, no," said Thor, "but the world's apparently pretty hosed no matter what happens. Might as well at least try to do the right thing."

"It's about fucking time you grew a pair," said Judy, sitting on the concierge desk. "The helicopter's just been wasting fuel out there."

Sixty-Seven: Sin City

Quetzalcoatl sat atop the facsimile Eiffel Tower, overlooking the burning ruins of Las Vegas, his tail coiled around the latticework of the tower's uppermost spire. Phil and Bill sat precariously on either side of him, without tails and huddled against the spire, whimpering slightly.

"It's beautiful, isn't it?" asked Quetzalcoatl.

"The neon... contrasted against the... inky darkness of night?" replied Phil. "I suppose it does have a certain... aesthetic quality that some might..."

"I meant all the burning prostitutes."

"Oh."

Las Vegas had not been in ruins or on fire until shortly after Quetzalcoatl arrived. It had, in fact, been the most prosperous city in the world from the third apocalypse onward. If there was one thing people loved to do during the end of the world, it was panic. If there was another, it was fuck. And if there was a third, it was gamble away their children's college funds while doing the first two.

"Do we have to... sit up here, Quetzalcoatl?" asked Bill, searching for something to hold on to. "It's quite... high."

"No," said Quetzalcoatl, "of course not."

Quetzalcoatl pushed Bill off the edge of the Eiffel Tower.

"What... Why would..." stammered Phil.

"Quiet," replied Quetzalcoatl, peering downward, "he hasn't hit the ground yet."

Phil's grip on the tower doubled in intensity. So did his heartbeat, the fear in his eyes, the certainty he was going to die, and his regret at never buying a parachute or learning how to fly.

"Oh, there we go. Landed on a Japanese guy. They are never going to get that out of the sidewalk."

The latticework dug deeply enough into Phil's hand to draw blood.

"So, anyway," said Quetzalcoatl, "I'm sure you're wondering why I've asked you up here this evening."

Phil responded by staring blankly in abject terror.

"Well, at least tell me you understand the gravity of the situation…"

Nothin'.

"C'mon, quit being such a dick, Phil. I'm trying to have a conversation here."

It took a few minutes, but Phil eventually remembered how to breathe regularly again. Then he remembered he was sitting atop a half-scaled Eiffel Tower with a sociopathic Aztec god in the middle of a burning city and had to go through the whole gamut of physiological responses to panic all over again.

The cycle repeated itself a few times, actually.

"You done?" asked Quetzalcoatl.

Phil responded with, "Buh…"

"That's still more syllables than you've given me in the last hour. I'm willing to call it a win. Let's get down to business."

"Guh…"

"Look, Phil, I love you, but I'm not in love with you. I carried your ass up here to talk strategy. If it wasn't for you and your… people, I might not be here right now. I figure I at least owe it to you to hear your opinion before I go ahead and do whatever I damn well please anyway. But if you're not actually going to contribute, you can just as easily join Bill down on the street."

"No, no. Strategy good," elocuted Phil. "What's… the plan?"

"Well, for starters, I'm thinking we should probably burn down the world."

"I'm… I'm sorry?"

"It really doesn't get any simpler than that, Phil."

"Why would we… burn down the world? I thought we were trying to… save it from itself… free it from the greed and the…

bureaucracy. I thought we were… giving society hope… an open-ended future…"

"Yeah, about that…"

"Even… even if you don't… if your goals…" continued Phil, his synapses not firing quite as quickly as they probably should have been. "Murdering everyone just doesn't seem productive."

Quetzalcoatl pushed Phil off the Eiffel Tower.

"I don't know," said Quetzalcoatl, "I seem to be producing corpses with surprising efficiency."

Quetzalcoatl looked from side to side and shrugged.

"Of course, now I'm sitting up here talking to myself," he continued. "I must look crazy."

Sixty-Eight: Elegy

"Well," thought Phil, as he plummeted toward his imminent, sidewalk-splattered doom, "this is it."

"Thrown off a faux French monument in the middle of a city in the middle of a desert in the middle of the night," he continued thinking, "by a newly re-deified deity intent on scorching the Earth for as mercurial and ill-defined a reason as revenge.

"Honestly, I did not see it coming."

Phil continued plummeting.

"It really is beautiful, though. The night, the city. Even the burning prostitutes. Their panic and continued flailing seem almost choreographed. It's majestic, in its own way. If only I had noticed earlier. Well, not the hookers, per se, but the... beauty inherent in everything. I know I wanted to, but I was trying so hard to get others to think of me the way I wanted to be thought of, trying so hard to make them believe that I could see the angels in everyone, that I completely failed to actually see them. I suppose wanting to be something isn't the same as actually being something. It's remarkably simple, really, astoundingly... apt, then, that by simply not trying, by not overanalyzing the approach, that by, quite literally and unfortunately, falling into it, I'm now able to accomplish the task."

Phil sighed deeply and continued his fall. He began ruminating on, and, for once, truly appreciating, the beauty of everything he could see from his peculiar vantage point: the neon-lit sky, the latticework rushing past him, the ever-approaching sidewalk.

Really, the sidewalk was quite lovely. Laid out in perfect lines, each square clean and unbroken. A kind of whitish-grey, with a stucco-like facing. A stucco-like facing Phil's face was rapidly nearing.

"Oh, sweet fucking fuckity fuck."

Phil tried to turn his body in mid-air, only getting as far as changing his jackknife into a belly-flop. He continued the metaphor by hooking his arms and attempting to swim himself out of danger.

It didn't help.

"I don't want to die I don't want to die I don't want to die"

That didn't really help either.

"Sweet merciful crap, I wish I believed in a god. Or that there were gods to believe in to begin with. Other than the one who just killed me, I mean. If only... Oh shit, sidewalk!"

Phil curled up as best he could and shielded his face from the oncoming ground.

Sixty-Nine: Deus ex Girlfriend

Phil waited for the impact. His body was tensed, his eyes were closed. Mentally, he had devolved from pleading for mercy into an endless string of expletives. The only thing close to a thought he had left was the vague hope that he didn't soil himself prior to becoming one with the pavement.

Phil continued to wait. His body was still tensed, although his feet were starting to feel pretty comfortable. Likewise, his brain eased up for the briefest of moments, squeezing out, "These last few seconds certainly are taking a good long while to pass," in between the frenzied cussing.

Phil waited a little while longer. Hesitantly, he opened his eyes and peered through the fingers still clenched around his face. He was expecting to see Heaven, or Hell, or maybe Quetzalcoatl holding his ankle and laughing, or about eight hundred equally as unlikely scenarios.

"What… the…?" said Phil.

Nowhere on that list was there a squirrel.

"Don't be alarmed," said the squirrel. "My name is Timmy."

Yet that's what Phil was looking at. A squirrel. An atypical, extraordinary, preternaturally intelligent, telekinetic, cape-wearing squirrel.

"You can… talk?"

"Do you see my lips moving?"

"Well, no."

"Right. Squirrels don't have vocal chords. I'm communicating with you the same way I'm holding you three inches from the ground: *with my brain*. Quit being such a fucking idiot."

There was a time when Timmy was just like any other squirrel. But there was this other time where he got experimented on and gained telekinetic powers. And then there was this third time where Timmy almost got hit by a car but, at the last second, pulled a rock from the side of the road and into harm's way, thus saving his ass and, surely, causing the inhabitants of the car, and anyone else somehow privy to the goings-on of said car, to believe that he had been run over. But he hadn't.

Instead, Timmy lived, and decided to use his newfound ass-saving abilities for the good of the world. He started small, avenging mistreated animals and the like, before quite literally moving his way up the food-chain, always searching for the bigger picture, the best way to help the most creatures.

Which is why when an overweight philosopher fell past Timmy as he climbed up a faux French monument in Las Vegas en route to killing Quetzalcoatl, Timmy didn't even blink.

Saving lives was just what Timmy did.

Seventy: Fun with Adjectives

"Thanks," said Phil, repositioning himself so that his feet were on the ground and his body was once more aligned with the vertical plane.

"Don't mention it," replied Timmy telepathically. "Now, if you'll excuse me, I've got bigger fish to psychokinetically eviscerate."

"He's actually a snake. With wings."

"Yeah, I know, I saw the reports on TV. It was just a play on words."

"Oh, right," said Phil, "right. Sorry, it's been a... hectic... disorientating couple of days."

"Been there, brother."

A helicopter noisily passed over the duo. They looked up, neither one entirely sure of what to expect. What they saw was Quetzalcoatl also noticing the helicopter and fleeing from the Eiffel Tower like a startled pigeon.

"Damn it," said Timmy, watching his prey escape.   "What the shit is that?" he asked, returning his attention to the flying machine.

"A helicopter," answered Phil.

"You have no idea how much I'm regretting saving your life."

The helicopter landed in the middle of the street, less than twenty yards from Phil and Timmy. A number of people in suits and a number of people not in suits poured from the vehicle's door.

"It's a philosopher!" shouted one of the ones in a suit, pointing at Phil. "Kill him!"

"Seriously," said Timmy. "No idea."

"Whoa, hold on," shouted Phil, stepping forward and putting up his hands in a gesture of surrender. "I'm... on your side."

"Why should we believe you?" said the suit with a bag on her head, approaching the duo.

"Because Quetzalcoatl... no longer cares for my company. He threw me... off the top of an Eiffel Tower."

"*An* Eiffel Tower?" asked a taller, bagless her.

The even taller, well-built man with the sideburns standing next to her pointed up.

"Oh, right," replied the girl.

"How are you alive then?" asked the other, shorter, bagless female.

"This squirrel..." said Phil, motioning to Timmy, "halted my descent... with his mind."

"Somehow," said the girl, lowering her head and rubbing her temples, "that's not the strangest thing I've ever heard."

Timmy stood up on his hind legs and waved. His tiny cape billowed heroically.

"Good enough for me," said the tall, blonde man by the girl's side, shrugging.

Seventy-One: If the Helicopter's A-Rockin'...

Judy and the other, suited scientists hung in the middle of the air, clutching their own throats and gasping out vague apologies.

"And that," said Chester A. Arthur XVII, "is good enough for me. I believe them."

"OK, Timmy," said Phil. "You can... let them down now."

"Do I have to?" replied the squirrel, speaking telepathically to everyone. "They are scientists, after all."

"Yes," said Catrina, "but they're not your scientists. This is a whole other group of incompetent scientists. While they are clearly, and very, stupid, they're not exactly evil. They don't deserve to be choked to death."

"Are you sure?" asked Thor.

"How is that helpful?"

"I'm just saying, they did nearly kill us."

"Thor."

"That thing? With the giant werewolf? Remember?"

Catrina shot Thor a look that would have killed a lesser man. Seriously. Dude would've burst into flames right there.

"OK, fine," replied Thor, rolling his eyes.

Thor knelt before Timmy and put both of his hands on the squirrel's tiny shoulders. He took a deep breath and looked Timmy squarely in his rodent eyes.

"Timmy," he said, "please do not kill these scientists. We apparently need them for some reason, maybe. More importantly, though, they are not very good at being scientists. They will undoubtedly find some way to kill themselves in a hilarious fashion shortly."

Timmy returned Thor's gaze, hesitation apparent in his eyes.

"Trust me," said Thor.

Timmy took a deep breath.

"OK," replied the caped super-squirrel, releasing the scientists from his telekinetic stranglehold. They fell to the ground with a variety of thuds.

"All right, well, with that out of the way, I guess it's time to start talking renegade Aztec gods," said Queen Victoria XXX.

"Makes sense," said Chester A. Arthur XVII. "What do you know, Phil?"

"You guys all right?" asked William H. Taft XLII, offering his hand to Judy.

"Oh my god," said Judy. "I am so turned on."

"Wait, what?"

"Well, I only met him for the first time... a couple weeks ago," said Phil.

Judy turned to her scientist companions saying, "Someone needs to do me, right the hell now."

She grabbed one by the arm and began pulling him toward the helicopter.

"You, let's go."

"He was... different then than he is now," continued the philosopher.

Judy shoved the scientist into the helicopter, climbed in on top of him, and slid the door shut.

"The wings are new, for one."

"Seriously, guys," said William H. Taft XLII, "did nobody else just see that?"

"The tail, as well."

"It just seems really inappropriate is all," continued the former president, scratching the back of his head. "And, you know, kinda creepy."

Seventy-Two: Boom

"Sir," said the completely nondescript bureaucratic drone whose fortune-telling mother hadn't even bothered to name him due to his fated role in the world, "it appears that Quetzalcoatl and his army have breached Las Vegas and destroyed most of the city."

"Damn it," said the President of the Amalgamated Provinces and States of Canada, America and Mexico, pounding his fist against his desk. "The hookers?"

"At half capacity, sir."

"Half?!" replied the president. "Our economy is ruined."

"Yes, sir."

"What about the Giant Killers?" asked the president, rubbing his forehead. "Do we have an ETA on them yet?"

"The Giant Killers, sir?"

"Operation Giant Killer?"

"None of the paperwork had 'Giant Killer' written on it," said the drone, flipping through the reports and files he was carrying.

"Well, no, it wouldn't. It was a *secret* plan."

"I don't know that there's anything particularly secret about this, sir," said the drone, still flipping. "Thor is referred to by name several times. As are his co-workers and the political clones who joined them. Political clones that don't legally exist. It's even got the model number and flight path of the helicopter taking them from New Jersey to Nevada. There is absolutely no part of this plan that uses any kind of discretion."

"Yeah," said the president, "that's not Operation Giant Killer."

"Sir?"

"I'm not really sure what you're looking at, son," explained the president. "The paperwork I got says I'm supposed to send in the Horsemen to deal with our little god infestation."

"The Horsemen? The Horsemen were ruled a crime against humanity, sir. By a court of clinically psychopathic criminals.

They were supposed to have been dismantled, melted down, turned into spoons, wrapped in plastic, and then fired into space," said the nameless drone, outrage quickly rising within him.

"Well, that proved to be expensive," said the president, "so they weren't."

"The Horsemen don't have filters, sir. They'll kill everyone."

"These things happen," he shrugged.

"Those people are innocent, sir. In fact, *you* dragged them into this. They're under *your* orders to try and save the world! You can't seriously do this."

"Actually," said the president, "I already did. I authorized the release of the Horsemen twenty minutes ago."

"Although," he continued, "I had forgotten how highly illegal that endeavor was, so I guess maybe you're right after all. Something should probably be done."

"Thank you for coming to your senses, sir," replied the nameless young man. "I really wasn't looking forward to all the paperwork I'd have to file in order to report this to the United Global Congressional Federation of Countries."

"Neither was I," replied the president, pulling a crossbow from his desk.

"Sir," said the completely nondescript bureaucratic drone whose fortune-telling mother hadn't even bothered to name him due to his fated role in the world, "what are you doing?"

"Solving our paperwork problem," replied the president as he loaded his crossbow.

"There are numerous, far better options..."

The President of the Amalgamated Provinces and States of Canada, America and Mexico shot an arrow into his assistant's chest.

"Too bad your mother never saw that coming."

"Actually, sir," said the nameless young man, looking down at the arrow sticking out of his sternum, "she did."

He slumped down into the armchair across from the president's desk.

"They'll probably blame you for this, you know."

"Blame me for what?" said the increasingly confused attempted murderer, loading another arrow.

The office drone opened his shirt to reveal a vest, a belt, and a bandolier, all loaded with, and made of, explosives.

"The fall of the Amalgamated Provinces and States of Canada, America and Mexico, for one," said the drone, beginning to spit up blood.

"I thought your torso was oddly shaped," said the president, shooting the office worker in the chest again.

"Consolidating all the government offices into one building was a pretty stupid idea."

The president shot the drone in the chest a third time.

"Especially considering how terrible a president you are, sir," continued the drone, blood pouring down his chin.

"No kidding, son," said the president. "I didn't even vote for me."

The president shot his assistant a fourth time.

"Are... are you done yet?" asked the drone, drifting from consciousness.

"Yeah," said the president, looking sadly at the empty crossbow. "There's a chainsaw in the closet, though..."

"Yeah, don't... don't bother," said the young man, lifting himself from the chair, stumbling, vomiting blood onto the president's carpet, and then collapsing back into the chair.

"You all right there, son?"

The completely nondescript bureaucratic drone whose fortune-telling mother hadn't even bothered to name him due to his fated role in the world raised an eyebrow and gave the president a look, then pulled a detonator from his pocket and pushed the button.

"Fuck you, sir."

Seventy-Three: Join, or Die

Quetzalcoatl stood—or coiled, or whatever it's called when a snake rests on his tail and gives a speech—before his gathered minions in the hollowed out remains of the Bellagio casino.

"Assorted smelly people in my employ…"

"You're not paying us," shouted Jill from the back of the crowd.

"I'm not charging you, though. Think of all that money you're not giving to me and consider it your earnings."

"I don't think…" said Jack, standing at Jill's side.

"I know you don't," said Quetzalcoatl, cutting him off. "And that's OK. We don't pass judgment on the mental shortcomings of others here."

"Speaking of stupid people within our ranks," continued Quetzalcoatl, "it's come to my attention that some of you may be wavering in your belief of me. Rest assured, I am still one hundred percent committed to whatever it is I told you I believed."

"World peace," said one member of the congregation.

"The dismantling of the patriarchy," corrected a second.

"Puppies!" shouted a third.

"Exactly," said Quetzalcoatl. "And I know some of you are also questioning just how and why things got so violent in the general areas I was inhabiting at any given time. The thing about that was, it wasn't. You're simply not opening your minds to their… openest. It wasn't violence at all; it was performance art! The flames you see engulfing this city are the literal interpretation of our ideas setting the world on fire."

"But," said Hil, "isn't that exactly the opposite way a metaphor is supposed to work?"

"Well, they'd clearly be expecting that, wouldn't they? Metaphorical burning is so played out."

A large portion of the crowd began nodding in approval. The ones who didn't—Hil and Jill included—furrowed their brows instead. Quetzalcoatl noticed this mass furrowing and addressed their concerns directly.

"If that still doesn't convince you to do what I say, just remember that I will kill you all without even a second thought."

The furrowed eyebrow to raised eyebrow ratio shifted significantly.

"Where are Bill and Phil?" asked one particularly swift and observant member of the Quetzalcoatl fan club.

"Not here," replied Quetzalcoatl. "Turns out neither of them could fly."

The raised eyebrow percentage skyrocketed, as did the angle of the raised eyebrows in question.

"More importantly, though, gentlemen and ladies, is that gathering of people not on fire over there," continued Quetzalcoatl, making his way to the far side of what passed for a room and pointing through the broken wall in the direction of the Eiffel Tower.

"That is a state of being that needs to be corrected."

Seventy-Four: Probably Not, No

"That's great and all," said Thor, "but how do we kill Quetzalcoatl?"

"Violence?" suggested Phil. "I don't really know."

"Seriously, man? That's your answer?"

"You've been at his side this entire time," added Chester A. Arthur XVII, "and that's all you've got?"

"Quetzalcoatl told me he once... destroyed a continent, but didn't die. Then he drowned... without actually drowning. Immediately after that... he drank himself into a coma... without actually going into a coma," said Phil.

"But, then, that was only his own... recounting of his history," he continued. "All I know with... certainty... is that last week, no more than ten feet from me, I watched him die... at the sharpened metal hands of a squadron of murder-drones. Only Quetzalcoatl didn't die. Instead, he... metamorphosed into... the winged snake god of a long-dead civilization.

"So, yes," Phil concluded, "nothing is all I've got."

"This is insane," said Queen Victoria XXX. "Everyone's got some kind of weakness, something that can be exploited. No soft underbelly? Allergies? He have a girlfriend or a daughter we can kidnap? A favorite teddy bear we can set on fire? Anything?"

"Even when he was being... straightforward, it sounded like he was speaking in riddles. Quetzalcoatl has no... allegiances, no... vulnerabilities that I've ever witnessed. I honestly don't know what else I can tell you."

"Uh, guys," interrupted William H. Taft XLII, "can you argue faster? I think Quetzalcoatl just found us."

He pointed to the incoming waves of angry liberal arts majors and hobos crowding the avenue and stretching back to the horizon. It was like a protest march for animal rights, only instead of signs, everyone was carrying axes and guns and weaponized pieces of murder-drone.

"Phil?" asked Catrina, facing the other direction and backing up into the center of the group. "When did you guys get killer robots?"

She pointed to the dozen truck-sized automatons marching in from the other end of the street.

"We didn't," said Phil, eyes growing wide.

"Oh, this won't end well," said William H. Taft XLII.

Seventy-Five: Five Weeks, Tops

After the world was ended for the sixth time—back when the occasional society-decimating cataclysm was still considered a problem—a team of Army engineers set out to end the end of the world once and for all. After performing several months' worth of math in several days, and drinking several dozen gallons of military-grade coffee, they concluded the most effective way to stop any future Armageddons was to hunt down and kill the Four Horsemen of the Apocalypse.

To do this, the engineers created twelve Horsemen of their own, each the size of a large Army personnel transport and resembling a centaur—assuming the viewer was either an eight-year old with an overactive imagination or eating mushrooms.

The Horsemen were over-armored, loaded with two of every weapon known to mankind, and programmed with a stripped-down, African-warlord version of the standard murder-drone programming. They were put through a rigorous, dedicated training regimen, but kept veering off-program and targeting live kittens instead. A few of the more even-headed engineers considered scrapping the program entirely prior to launch, but they were all mysteriously set on fire.

"I think I can... talk the philosophers out of this," said Phil. "I don't know what you're going to do about... them, though," he continued, indicating the walking war-crimes.

"I can take 'em," said Timmy.

The Horsemen were successful in murdering the Four Horsemen of the Apocalypse. After a meteor strike ended the world for the seventh time, it became apparent that they had been significantly less successful in actually stopping any apocalypses. This made the Horsemen mad.

"Are you fucking crazy?" asked Catrina.

The Horsemen weren't actually supposed to be capable of anger, but, due to a misplaced one in the Horsemen's coding, they were able to work themselves into a rage on the same level as an old-money douchebag with an overdeveloped sense of entitlement forced to wait in a line of perfectly reasonable length.

"Nope," replied Timmy. "Just awesome."

The Horsemen went on a rampage and murdered half the world's population. They were only stopped after Japan built a team of brightly-colored robots shaped like jungle cats. The Japanese robots actually failed to stop the Horsemen the first three times, but then they were reconfigured to connect into one other and given a great, big sword and then the world was saved. Well, eventually it was. The battle actually sank Japan and ended the world for the eighth time. But then, then the world was saved. For, like, a month.

Seventy-Six: It'd Take a Miracle

"OK," said Chester A. Arthur XVII. "Billy, you take the scientists and go with Phil."

"Sure thing," said William H. Taft XLII.

"I don't know what good... scientists are going to do against... righteous, riled-up writers and poets," replied Phil.

"That's why I'm sending Billy," said Chester A. Arthur XVII.

"I... fail to see how that adds anything to the mix."

"Let me clarify: That's why I'm sending Billy and his rocket launcher."

"Oh," said Phil. "Right, then."

"Hey," said Judy, putting her hand on Chester A. Arthur's shoulder and spinning him to face her, "who says you get to call the shots?"

"I do," replied Chester A. Arthur XVII coolly.

"OK, then," she replied, removing her hand from his shoulder and nodding her bag.

"Let's go 'talk' to these assholes," said William H. Taft XLII, hoisting his rocket launcher.

"Can you try... not to kill them... if you don't have to?" asked Phil.

"No promises."

"Some of them... are my friends."

"Man, that's your problem."

The president, the philosopher, and the scientists left the other president, the queen, the god, and the girl, and walked towards the encroaching horde of liberal arts majors and drug dealers.

"All right, now, Timmy..." said Chester A. Arthur XVII, turning his attention toward the Horsemen.

"Already gone, bitch," replied the telepathic squirrel from half a mile away.

"Right, well, good luck then," thought the president in return.

"I don't need luck, chump."

"If you say so. When you're getting stomped on by ten foot tall robotic sadists, don't blame me."

"Says the non-scientifically-enhanced human tasked with taking down an ancient, insane, robot-smashing god."

"I was trying not to think about it in terms quite like that, so, you know, thanks for that," answered Chester A. Arthur XVII. "Get out of my head."

"With pleasure," replied Timmy.

"Why is he just standing there?" asked Thor, pointing a thumb at Chester A. Arthur XVII.

"Maybe he's strategizing or something," offered Catrina.

"That's not his strategizing face," said Queen Victoria XXX. "That's his 'I can't believe I'm being taunted by a rodent' face."

"He has a face specifically for that?"

"Yeah," replied the queen with a sigh. "There's also one for particularly contentious cacti."

"This happens so much more than it should," she added.

After a few more moments of arguing with the genetically-modified squirrel, Chester A. Arthur XVII spoke aloud again.

"OK, there are four of us and one of him…"

"That's his strategizing face," said Queen Victoria XXX.

"…so if we spread out, each take a compass direction, we should be able to track him down with a fair amount of ease."

"Although," he continued, "the giant robots aren't his."

"The giant robots blowing the living crap out of everything," added Catrina.

"That's also assuming he hasn't just bailed entirely," said Queen Victoria XXX.

A trio of burning prostitutes ran past.

"Shouldn't he be holed up in a castle or something?" asked Thor.

"I think you're thinking of Super Mario Bros., Thor," replied the queen.

"No," said Thor, "I'm pretty sure I read something some-where about how they always made their lairs in castles or something."

"They?"

"You're thinking of a dragon," said Catrina.

"Right..." said Thor, failing to see her point.

"He's not a dragon, Thor."

"Yeah, I know, but, he's like a dragon."

"OK," said Chester A. Arthur XVII, "anyone who isn't Thor have a suggestion?"

There was a loud bang from the side of the street—specifically, from a direction that did not appear to involve giant robots or a philosopher/scientist showdown and, in turn, probably should not have been making loud banging noises. Catrina, Chester, Thor and Victoria turned toward the source of the sound simultaneously, just in time to see Quetzalcoatl fly through the dust of a collapsing hotel and alight on the highest turret of the Excalibur casino. A casino that just happened to be shaped like a castle.

"Well, I'll be damned," said Chester A. Arthur XVII.

"Not unless Satan decided he was tired of not existing, too," replied Catrina.

"That motherfucker just took down an entire building by himself," said Queen Victoria XXX. "We are so screwed."

"Probably," said Thor, grabbing a flamethrower from the helicopter. "Let's go find out."

Seventy-Seven: Olive Branch

"Gil," said Phil, approaching the militant crowd of philosophers and poets, "what are you doing?"

"Honestly," said Gil, looking at the two-by-four he was carrying, "I don't even know anymore, man."

"Quetzalcoatl, like, he told us to kill you, man," said Lil.

"Well, actually," clarified Hil, scratching her head with the tire iron she was holding, "he told us that he already killed *you* and that we were supposed to kill *him*," she pointed the tire iron at William H. Taft XLII, "and his friends."

"Or else he'd kill us," added Jill.

"It was just bad juju all around, man," said Gil.

The writers and stoners and assorted other nouns standing behind the conversing members appeared to just be milling around, staring at their feet or otherwise looking confused and sad.

A few had taken the halt in marching to mean it was time to sit down and stare off into space. A few others had been doing that even before the group had stopped walking.

"Seriously?" said William H. Taft XLII, looking over the crowd. "This was your philosopher army?"

"Yep," said Phil.

"I can't believe you guys actually took over half the country," said the president. "Honestly. How'd he get you guys out of your parents' basements?"

"My mom doesn't get around so well, man," said Gil, a downhearted look on his face.

"Yeah," said Lil, putting an arm around Gil, "That's a little harsh, man."

"We were just trying to do some good," said Jill.

"It's not our fault we picked a dormant Aztec god as our spiritual leader," added Jack.

"Actually, it kind of is," countered William H. Taft XLII.

"Well, yeah, OK," said Hil. "But he seemed less evil earlier."

"In our defense," added Phil, "he was a pretty good liar."

"All right, well," said William H. Taft XLII, "if you promise to drop your weapons and not kill me and my friends, I'll apologize."

The members at the forefront of the group acquiesced immediately, while the remainder only did so when the offer was passed back to them. Eventually, the entire philosopher army dropped its weapons, a slow-moving wave of clanks and thuds and sighs of relief.

Also, they did not kill William H. Taft XLII or his friends.

"OK, then," said the president. "I'm sorry. I guess."

"It's all right, man," said Gil.

"Yeah, it's OK, man," said Lil. "We forgive you."

She took a step closer to the president, opening her arms and saying, "C'mon, let's hug it out."

"Do we have to?" said William H. Taft XLII.

Lil hugged him ferociously.

"See," she said, squeezing the fat man, "doesn't that feel good?"

"I feel so dirty."

Seventy-Eight: A Tiny, Steaming Load

Timmy was a squirrel. An atypical, extraordinary, preternaturally intelligent, telekinetic, cape-wearing squirrel. Gifted with artificial sentience and a super-powered mind, he swore an oath to make the world a better place.

The Horsemen—engines of pure destruction born from the folly of mankind—marched down the avenue in four rows of three, firing missiles and lasers and large rocks indiscriminately. Flames spouted from their metallic nostrils. Death followed them like a fine, dark mist.

Well, to be fair, Timmy never really *swore* anything. He just kind of did it. There was certainly no oath, anyway.

Although he did tell the reconstituted genetics of a former president that he was going to stop the Horsemen single-handedly. And that is a promise that simply cannot be broken.

Seriously, death followed the Horsemen like a fine, dark mist. Everything behind them was broken, vaporized, and reduced to subatomic dust.

Well, OK, it could be broken, but that wouldn't really be cool. If nothing else, Timmy was a squirrel of his word.

Everything in front of the Horsemen was exploding. Even the air. Individual molecules were screaming in agony, praying in vain for the sweet release of nonexistence.

But what are words, really...
    No. No. He was doing this. Timmy was doing this.

A cockroach scuttled in front of the Horsemen's path. The lead Horseman whinnied—an awful, terrible sound—and reared up on its back two legs, before bringing its full weight down on the cockroach.

Then the other eleven horsemen did the same thing.

Then they all fired lasers at the insect, not stopping until the pavement beneath what used to be the cockroach was boiling itself away into the ether.

Timmy was a squirrel. An atypical, extraordinary, preternaturally intelligent, telekinetic, cape-wearing squirrel that just dropped a load in the middle of the street.

Seventy-Nine: Boss Fight

Thor, Catrina, Chester A. Arthur XVII, and Queen Victoria XXX, heavily armed and more or less determined, walked down the street, stepping over the occasional dead tourist or twitching brochure-hawker, and made their way to the casino.

Quetzalcoatl saw their approach and waved from his perch.

"He seems nice," said Queen Victoria XXX.

"What, uh, what do we do now?" asked Catrina confusedly. "Call him out? Throw a rock?"

"I've got a better idea," said Chester A. Arthur XVII, shouldering a rocket-propelled grenade launcher. The president aimed at the Aztec god and pulled the trigger. The projectile hit Quetzalcoatl in the face and exploded.

"Aren't you supposed to add some kind of witty taunt to that?" asked Thor.

"I thought I did."

"Well, that was kind of oblique, you know? I was thinking something more direct, like, 'knock, knock, bitch.'"

"That doesn't really seem like something I would say, though."

"I don't know. I think you could pull it off."

"You sure? I'm really more of a speech guy."

"Uh, guys," said Catrina, pointing toward a swooping and pissed off Quetzalcoatl, "shut up and do something."

"Fuck."

Quetzalcoatl slammed into the ground with tremendous force, shattering the sidewalk beneath him. The shockwave knocked the girls to the ground, while the reborn god's whipping tail caught Thor at the knee and spun him face-first into the pavement. Chester A. Arthur XVII, however, managed to remain standing. He raised his RPG, only to remember it was unloaded.

"Fuck!"

Quetzalcoatl slammed his fist into Chester's face, breaking his nose and sending him sprawling across the sidewalk.

"Knock, knock, bitches," said Quetzalcoatl.

"Oh, come on," said Thor, picking himself up from the ground. "That was ours! It doesn't even fit what you're doing."

"I was knocking you guys on your asses, it totally fit."

"That's stretching it, man," explained Thor, pointing the igniter of his flamethrower at Quetzalcoatl and pulling the trigger. "See, right now, I'm setting you on fire. So what I'm going to do is make some kind of crack about the heat. Or grilling. Something like, 'I hope you like your gods well done.' Or maybe, 'I don't know where I'm going to find a tortilla big enough for this,' since you're Mexican and all. Although that might be a little too racially insensitive, I'm not really sure."

"I'm cool with it," said Quetzalcoatl, shrugging and being doused in flames.

"Oh, good," said Thor. "I kind of like that one."

"You mind terribly if I tried again?"

"Knock yourself out."

"OK," said Quetzalcoatl, still being bathed in a jet of flame. "How about, 'Tell the electricians I said "hi."'"

"Well, no, see, that's actually worse. There're no electricians here, it makes even less sense."

Quetzalcoatl pointed toward the building on the far side of the casino's property, specifically the marquee stating "West Coast Construction Workers Conference" in tall, bright, easily-read letters.

"Crap," said Thor, extinguishing the flamethrower. "Nice one."

"I thought so."

In a single, astoundingly quick motion, Quetzalcoatl slid his way to Thor's side, grabbed him by the face, and pushed, sending Thor sailing over the Excalibur's entranceway and through the window of the neighboring convention hall.

Eighty: With a Cool, Dry Wit Like That...

"So, with that out of the way," said Quetzalcoatl, making his way toward Catrina and Queen Victoria XXX, "who wants to get eaten first?"

"Oh my god, you eat people?" asked Queen Victoria XXX.

"I don't want to get eaten," said Catrina.

Quetzalcoatl laughed.

"I don't eat people, it's OK."

He grabbed a chunk of broken cement from the ground before clarifying, "I am going to kill you, though. Probably with this piece of sidewalk. Please don't be mistaken about that."

"Well," said Catrina, pulling two .44 Magnums from behind her back, "you can certainly try."

She unloaded twelve rounds directly into Quetzalcoatl's face. Quetzalcoatl's head snapped back. Then it snapped forward. The he blinked a few times.

"Really? A handgun?"

"No," said Queen Victoria XXX, also pulling two .44s from behind her back, "a number of handguns."

She likewise unloaded twelve rounds directly into Quetzalcoatl's face. Once again, Quetzalcoatl's head snapped back, then forward, and then he blinked.

"What is wrong with you people?"

A rocket-propelled grenade exploded in Quetzalcoatl's face.

"Clearly not our aim," said Chester A. Arthur XVII.

"Seriously, fucking stop. You guys are not Bruce Willis."

Quetzalcoatl's lip was bleeding slightly. He put his finger on the cut, pulled it away, and then looked at it so he could verify this fact for himself.

"And now I bit my lip. Great."

"If it bleeds," said Queen Victoria XXX, "we can kill it."

"No. No, no, no, no. You seriously did not just say that, did you?"

"I didn't not say it, jerkface."

"You turkeys might as well be juggling Jell-O for all you've accomplished," said Quetzalcoatl, putting down the sidewalk he had been brandishing. "Go ahead, shoot me again."

"I'm sorry?" asked Queen Victoria XXX, raising an eyebrow.

"Shoot me again."

"Which one of us?"

"All of you," said Quetzalcoatl, "at once."

"Seriously?" asked Catrina.

"Sure."

"OK," said Chester A. Arthur XVII with a shrug. "Your funeral."

"Yeah," said Quetzalcoatl, "I kind of doubt that."

Catrina, Queen Victoria XXX, and Chester A. Arthur XVII reloaded their weapons. They drew a bead on Quetzalcoatl's face. Quetzalcoatl smiled sweetly. A flaming prostitute ran screaming in between them, fell over, got up, and continued running down the street. Everyone looked at everyone else, shrugged, and then resumed the standoff.

"On the count of three, girls," said Chester A. Arthur XVII. "One…"

"Two…" added Quetzalcoatl.

"Three."

Catrina, Queen Victoria XXX, and Chester A. Arthur XVII fired directly into Quetzalcoatl's face from less than five feet away.

The explosion of the grenade caused Catrina, Victoria, and Chester to shield their faces, singing arm hair and throwing shrapnel in the process. Quetzalcoatl, however, never stopped smiling. He didn't even bother snapping his head back for dramatic effect this time around.

"Now, as you can quite plainly see," said Quetzalcoatl, his sweet, taunting grin becoming sinister and menacing, "I ain't got time to bleed."

He spread his wings and raised himself from the ground, towering over the trio, adding, "I think our little play date is over."

"Yippee-ki-yay, motherfucker!"

"OK, which of you said that?" asked Quetzalcoatl. "You're dying first."

"Who said what?" asked Catrina.

"I told you douchehorses no more action hero quipping."

"We didn't say anything," said Queen Victoria XXX.

"Don't you..."

Quetzalcoatl never finished his sentence. Or question. Or whatever it was. Instead, he was punched in the back of the head by a giant robot. A giant robot made up of other robots. More specifically, a giant robot cobbled together from the broken pieces of a dozen defeated Horsemen and piloted by a telekinetic squirrel in a cape. Quetzalcoatl was punched in the back of the head, by a robot made of other robots and piloted by a squirrel, with such tremendous force that not only his head, but his shoulders, as well, busted through the busted-up pavement and were now located in the packed dirt under the surface of the ground.

"Timmy!" squealed Catrina.

"Ma'am," replied the squirrel telepathically, manipulating his giant frankenrobot to tip an invisible hat toward the girl.

"You just saved our asses," said Queen Victoria XXX.

"Yeah," said Timmy, "funny how that works."

"We would have figured it out eventually," replied Chester A. Arthur XVII.

"Sure you would've."

Before Chester A. Arthur XVII could retort, Quetzalcoatl removed himself from the ground with great exuberance, spraying gravel and chunks of cement everywhere. He immediately resumed his earlier towering, menacing pose, albeit with significantly more emphasis on the menace this time around.

"OK, seriously," said the Aztec god, cracking his neck, "fuck all y'all."

Quetzalcoatl grabbed Timmy's robot contraption with his tail, slammed it into the already battered sidewalk, then into a pile of rubble that used to be a wall, then into a wall that was still a wall, and then flung Timmy and his machine into the stratosphere.

"Timmy!" cried Catrina.

In a single motion, Quetzalcoatl backhanded all three of his remaining assailants as they tried to load their weapons, simultaneously disarming them and sending them sprawling into the street. The snake god darted forward, pinning them all to the ground with his tail.

"This ends now," snarled Quetzalcoatl, leaning into the face of Chester A. Arthur.

"Like fuck it does, you maniacal assclown," shouted Queen Victoria XXX, struggling to remove Quetzalcoatl's tail from atop her legs.

Quetzalcoatl punched the sidewalk, the concrete splitting into a dozen or so pointed pieces. He grabbed one and plunged the shard into Victoria's abdomen.

"No," he said. "No more."

"Oh my god," said Catrina, "we've got to –"

"Get her medical attention? Yeah, that's not going to happen. I burned or knocked down every hospital within three miles," said Quetzalcoatl with a shrug. "I get bored."

Eighty-One: Hell Hath No Fury

"You fucking cocksucker," said Queen Victoria XXX.

"Yeah, that'll help, honey," replied Quetzalcoatl, still leaning over the trio. "Maybe you should try to think of something a little more family-friendly for your epitaph."

Queen Victoria XXX, her legs still pinned beneath Quetzalcoatl's tail, pulled the cement spike out of her gut.

"OK, um," said Quetzalcoatl, his menacing glare momentarily replaced by a look of confusion, "I wasn't aware anyone else here had any special powers."

"I don't," replied Queen Victoria XXX. "I'm bleeding to death and it hurts like a motherfucking bitch. But, powers or no…"

"…she is a vessel of fury and rage the likes of which you have never seen," continued Chester A. Arthur XVII, with far too smug a look on his face for someone with a giant snake resting on his chest.

Queen Victoria XXX stabbed Quetzalcoatl in the eye with the sidewalk splinter, bringing her arm around with enough force to shove the spike through the back of his skull.

Quetzalcoatl screamed and reeled backward, freeing the president, the queen, and the girl.

"Holy… FUCK, that fucking hurts," said Quetzalcoatl, absently grabbing at the concrete shard. "I really hope you don't have the HIV."

"Me too," said Thor, smacking Quetzalcoatl upside the head with a sledgehammer.

"Fucking hell, man!" exclaimed Quetzalcoatl. "Where the shit did you come from?"

"Convention let out early. Steve the electrician says 'hi.'"

Thor swung the sledgehammer upward, catching Quetzalcoatl by the chin and knocking him backward.

"Thor!" said Catrina, running up and embracing him.

"Catrina," said Thor. "How we doing?"

"Vicky's bleeding to death and Chester's not quite as pretty as he was, oh, and Timmy's an astronaut now, but, otherwise pretty good."

"Your definition of good leaves a lot to be desired," said Quetzalcoatl, regaining his ground and taking a swing at Thor.

Thor shielded Catrina and ducked out of the way. Chester A. Arthur XVII hit Quetzalcoatl across the face with a slab of sidewalk, sending him reeling backward.

"Nobody gives a shit what you have to say," said Chester A. Arthur XVII, bringing the piece of sidewalk down over Quetzalcoatl's head, "bitch."

"Hey, that is kind of fun," he added.

"Told you," said Thor.

Eighty-Two: Armageddon There

"By no pounds or Indians will some photosynthesizing chimp-neighbor buy up all my property, no ma'am," muttered Quetzalcoatl, picking himself off the ground once again.

"Is he insulting us or having a stroke?" asked Chester A. Arthur XVII.

"I don't know," said Thor, shaking his head, "and I don't really care."

He nodded to a pile of power tools and construction equipment by the curb and said, "I brought presents."

"I call the chainsaw!" said Catrina.

"Damn it," said Chester A. Arthur XVII and Queen Victoria XXX in unison.

"Oh, man," said Catrina, picking up the chainsaw, "this thing is heavy."

"Then let me take it," said Chester A. Arthur XVII, looking sadly at the nail-gun in his hand.

"Why?" countered Queen Victoria XXX. ""Cause you're a man and she's just a little girl?"

"What? No, that's not —"

"Then what, Charlie? What are you —"

The president looked at Catrina, struggling to start the gas-powered saw.

"I'm just saying, I've—we, we, you and me—have more experience in —"

"She's never going to learn if you keep treating her like —"

"I'm not treating her like anything! I was simply —"

"Uh, hurry up, guys," said Thor, taking a punch to the jaw from Quetzalcoatl. He retaliated by kicking Quetzalcoatl in the crotch, only to realize that Quetzalcoatl didn't have a crotch. The Aztec snake god pushed the off-balance Thor to the side.

"Chocolate-coated peanuts!"

"Oh, no," said Queen Victoria XXX, "I think we broke him."

Quetzalcoatl lunged at the queen. She side-stepped his attack and hit him in the back of the head with a pair of crowbars. He staggered slightly from the blow, long enough for Chester A. Arthur XVII to fire the nail-gun into his neck repeatedly.

"Son of a bitch!"

Quetzalcoatl swung blindly behind him. Chester A. Arthur XVII dodged the attack easily, then grabbed the Aztec god's hand and nailed it to the lower part of his back. Queen Victoria XXX cracked Quetzalcoatl across the face.

"Puppies, all of you!"

Quetzalcoatl extended his wings, knocking down both the president and the queen. He turned to lunge at Chester A. Arthur XVII, only to catch a sledgehammer from Thor with his teeth. The snake god fell backwards from the blow, landing against an up-turned slab of sidewalk. Chester A. Arthur XVII scrambled to his feet and fired the nail gun into Quetzalcoatl's shoulders, arms, and wings, pinning him to the slab.

"Catrina, take his head off," ordered the president. "Now."

Catrina pulled the cord urgently and the chainsaw roared to life. Still carrying it unsteadily, she took a step toward the Aztec god.

"OK, maybe, uh, maybe you were right," she said. "I don't know if I really feel comfortable doing this."

"Fine, whatever, I'll do it," said Chester A. Arthur XVII.

"Why –" started Queen Victoria XXX.

"Because I'm closer, Vicky," replied the president, shouting over his shoulder as he ran toward Catrina. "This is not the god damned time for this."

"Thanks," said Catrina, carefully handing over the chainsaw to the presidential clone.

Chester A. Arthur XVII reached out his hand, but was grabbed by Quetzalcoatl's tail before he could grab the saw. The snake god slammed the president into the side of the casino repeatedly, before impaling Chester on an exposed piece of metal.

"Charlie!" cried out Queen Victoria XXX, before turning and slashing her crowbars across the still-pinned Aztec god's face. She twirled the crowbars in her hands, adjusting her grip, and drove them both into Quetzalcoatl's chest.

Quetzalcoatl howled, then swung his tail back, catching Queen Victoria at the knees. He snapped his tail, changing its direction instantly and whipping it across the queen's face, gashing her cheek as she fell to the ground.

Thor stepped quickly toward Quetzalcoatl, raising the sledge-hammer. The Aztec god, wary of another blow to the face, picked Queen Victoria up off the ground and hurled her directly at Thor. The former god of thunder checked his swing and attempted to catch the queen, the two of them dropping to the ground in a tangle.

Quetzalcoatl struggled to free himself, absent-mindedly thrashing his tail at Catrina in the process.

"Oh shit," she said, lifting the chainsaw at the incoming tail.

Catrina held her ground, the teeth of the saw tearing into the writhing tail, but it was a futile defense. Quetzalcoatl freed himself from the slab and darted to the girl's side, grabbing Catrina by the neck. The chainsaw fell to the ground.

"I am going to murder you... and your children... and your goats."

"Put her down," said Thor, picking up his sledgehammer and limping toward Quetzalcoatl.

"You rock-skulled, rooster-smoking sack of liquids," replied the snake-man, "when are you going to learn? You can't kill me. I'm a *god*."

"Funny story," said Thor, tilting his head and cracking his neck, "so am I."

Eighty-Three: Ragnarok & Roll

Thor charged at Quetzalcoatl and, careful to avoid damaging Catrina, struck the Aztec god in the face with the sledgehammer. Quetzalcoatl just looked at him. Thor hit him a few more times. Quetzalcoatl remained unimpressed.

"Nope," he said. "Still gonna kill her."

Quetzalcoatl lifted Catrina, squeezing his fingers tighter around her neck. She began coughing and kicking her legs frantically.

"No," said Thor, "you're not."

The sky darkened as roiling, black clouds overtook the sun. A colossal crack of thunder echoed off what remained of the casino's walls, shaking the ground.

"Oh, no fucking way," said Quetzalcoatl.

A bolt of lightning tore through the sky, striking Quetzalcoatl. Catrina fell from his grasp.

"Holy shit, Thor," she said, stumbling towards him, "was –"

"Verily."

"But how? I thought –"

"Anything that prick can do," replied Thor, "I can do better."

"Yeah, well, anything I can do that you can do better I can do best," said Quetzalcoatl, picking himself off the ground yet again and coiling his tail to strike.

"Yeah," said Thor, "I kind of doubt that."

Catrina jumped to the side as Quetzalcoatl lunged at Thor. Thor hit him in the shoulder with the sledgehammer, sending the snake god sprawling sideways across the ground. Quetzalcoatl immediately launched himself at Thor again, but Thor caught him in the throat with his elbow.

Quetzalcoatl fell backwards, choking. Thor swung the sledge-hammer and struck Quetzalcoatl in the face, spinning and disorienting him. Thor capitalized and pummeled the snake-man mercilessly, lightning assaulting the Aztec god with each strike of the hammer. Quetzalcoatl swung blindly and thrashed futilely throughout the onslaught, never quite regaining his bearings, before a final blow to the square of his back sent Quetzalcoatl collapsing to the ground.

Thor gripped the sledgehammer with both hands and lifted it over his head. He swung it down onto Quetzalcoatl's skull with all his might. The accompanying thunder shattered windows, the bolt of lightning set the surrounding sidewalk on fire.

And then the sky cracked open.

"Oh, crap," said Thor.

Eighty-Four: The End

Queen Victoria XXX staggered over to Chester A. Arthur XVII and helped free him from the metal spike through the rightmost part of his chest.

"You all right?" she asked, gently helping to lift him.

"More than likely. I'm pretty sure it's not entirely fatal," said Chester A. Arthur XVII, wincing as he was removed from the exposed reinforcement bar. "How about you?"

"Bleeding profusely, but I'll probably live. I don't think he got anything important."

"That's good."

Queen Victoria XXX smiled. She lifted Chester's arm and put it around her shoulder, then the two of them attempted to stand. It was a valiant effort. They got about half way to vertical before falling backwards and landing on their asses.

"Maybe we should just sit here for..."

"Yeah..."

They sat there for a moment, surveying the wreckage and watching the blood pool around Quetzalcoatl's broken skull, before Victoria asked, "Where's Billy?"

"And Phil? And the scientists, for that matter?"

William H. Taft XLII and Phil, having dispersed the philosopher army, decided to rejoin their comrades in the dispatching of Quetzalcoatl. Before they could enter the fray, however, they came across a clutch of non-burning prostitutes trapped within a burning building. All hopped-up on being the good guys, William H. Taft XLII and Phil rescued the hookers from the building— well, a decent percentage of them, anyway—and brought them to safety.

They were still being rewarded for their heroism.

The scientists, however, having been less than useful in both the dispersal of the philosophers and the saving of the prostitutes, were not being rewarded. They were, nevertheless, still with Phil, William H. Taft XLII, and the hookers, just watching. Judy, especially, felt that was reward enough. She was kind of a weird girl.

"I hope they're OK," said Queen Victoria XXX.

"Where's the helicopter?" asked Chester A. Arthur XVII.

The helicopter was where they had left it.

"What's that matter? It's not like we can fly it without a pilot."

"Sure we can."

"You can fly a helicopter?"

"Well, no," replied Chester A. Arthur XVII. "But I'm a quick study."

"You're an idiot, Charlie."

Queen Victoria XXX and Chester A. Arthur XVII, each supporting the other one, lifted themselves from the ground with a deep breath and a heave. They began staggering back toward the helicopter when Catrina approached them.

"You guys OK?"

"We will be," said Queen Victoria XXX. "We're going to take the helicopter and find some help."

"Good idea," replied Catrina. "Good luck."

"Thanks," said Chester A. Arthur XVII. "We'll swing back here when we're done. If you're already gone, we'll meet you back at the hotel."

"Do you ever turn off?"

"No," replied Chester A. Arthur XVII with a smile.

Catrina waved at the president and the queen as they walked away. They turned a corner and Catrina turned to look for Thor. He was standing off to the side, leaning on his sledgehammer and staring at the roiling hole in the heavens. Catrina walked up to him.

"Well, shit," she said, also looking at the broken sky.

"Yup," said Thor.

"So, uh, assuming you're right," said Catrina, crowding closer to him, "what happens now?"

Thor put his arm around her and shrugged.

"The end of everything, I guess."

Epilogue: Thor, God of Terrible Predictions

"Hi, this is room 218. Can I have a few more pillows sent up?"

"Why? Were the pillows missing?"

"What? No, no. I'd just like a few more pillows."

"Why?"

"What do you mean 'why?'"

"I mean what the hell, man? No one needs that many damn pillows."

"Maybe I do."

"And maybe you're a jackass."

"That's no way to talk to a paying customer."

"I'll… It's…"

"Ha! That's right, Thor! Bring me my damn pillows!"

"You're such a tool, Charlie."

Thor hung up the phone, and then he hung his head.

"Asshole better take his time healing, 'cause I'm breaking some damn bones once he does," he muttered.

"Ease up, Thor," said Catrina. "He got a pole through his chest."

"Yeah, but he doesn't have to be such a douchebag about it."

"He's not being a douchebag. He's legitimately incapacitated."

"Legitimately incapacitated, my ass," replied the God of Thunder. "If you've got such a soft spot for him, why don't you go bring him his pillows?"

"Screw that, man," said Catrina, putting her feet up on the desk. "You answered the phone, not me. You do it."

"This is bullshit," he muttered as he walked out from behind the service desk.

About the Author:

Eirik Gumeny is not ashamed to admit that he's from New Jersey. He started writing at the tender age of five, when someone told him he had to, probably. He is the proud owner of an English degree from Montclair State University, which has opened many doors for him. Mostly at call centers. He's also been employed as an ice cream counter jockey, a video store clerk, a copy writer for dollar bin kung-fu flicks, and actually once attempted to sell completely ephemeral credit card processing contracts to bodegas in a predominately Spanish neighborhood despite the fact that he does not speak Spanish. He was told it wasn't a pyramid scheme, but he has his doubts.

Eirik has often been told his work is most likely influenced by drugs, an excessive intake of coffee, or a lack of sleep, but he'd prefer to blame Douglas Adams, Kurt Vonnegut, and Warren Zevon. Eirik's stories and poems have been published in a number of online literary journals, including "Boy Meets Girl" at Thieves Jargon, "The Astrophysicist" at the late Saucyvox, "Storybook Romance" at the equally as late Green Muse, "Caffeine" and "Hector & Sheila & Kevin" at Defenestration, "Bagel" at Monkeybicycle, and "Last Exit in New Jersey" at Mud Luscious, among others.

Eirik has never been awarded a Pushcart, nor has he been nominated for one. He's also never won a Nobel Prize, a Pulitzer, an Olympic medal, or the NFC East. He did win a camera at work once, though. When Eirik is not writing or daydreaming about being on his book tour with his girl-friend, he's probably asleep and actually dreaming about it. Or in his living room playing video games.

For more of Eirik's writing go to your computer and navigate your way to egumeny.blogspot.com. To offer him huge sums of money, email him at eirik.gumeny@gmail.com.

Acknowledgements:

Firstly, I'd like to mention that this book owes a great debt of gratitude to my job. Without the constant downtime and boredom, the story might not have started. And the constant stream of co-workers made it much easier to name my characters.

As well, I'd like to thank my professors in the English program at Montclair State. Specifically Dr. Nash, for laughing at my ridiculous take on non-fiction, and Prof. Lorenz, for encouraging me to keep this up.

Thanks to Uncle Paul, for giving me all those comics when I was naught but an impressionable youth.

Thanks to my family – Mom, Dad, Bryan, and Kristen – for innumerable reasons.

Thanks to Steve and Sarita, for constantly telling me I was better than I thought I was.

And thanks to Monica, for making me believe it.